FRIENDLY PERSUASION

Ki stepped away a pace, revolver leveled. "Now, answer me. What're they up to? What're their plans?"

"Señor, I know nothing. Nobody tells me—"

"Too bad." Ki thumbed back the gunhammer.

"*M-madre de Dios!*" Duron babbled, ogling the pistol. "I-there is talk, senor, talk of—"

A volley of gunshots blasted from the doorway. Duron fell out of the chair, dead before he landed on the floor.

Whirling in a crouch, Ki brought the pistol to bear—

"Fire," a voice snapped, "and we'll blow your brains out!"

◆► WESLEY ELLIS ◄◆

LONE STAR

AND THE
TEXAS KILLERS

J

JOVE BOOKS, NEW YORK

LONE STAR AND THE TEXAS KILLERS

A Jove Book / published by arrangement with
the author

PRINTING HISTORY
Jove edition / October 1989

ISBN: 0-515-10155-9

Jove Books are published by The Berkley Publishing Group,
200 Madison Avenue, New York, New York 10016.
The name "JOVE" and the "J" logo
are trademarks belonging to Jove Publications, Inc.

PRINTED IN THE UNITED STATES OF AMERICA

10 9 8 7 6 5 4 3 2 1

Chapter 1

It was an inferno of a summer, even for Texas.

All day the sun burned like hell's own branding iron, scaring the two riders who were heading south toward the Big Bend country. Following an eroded and rubble-strewn wagon track, they flanked Maravillas Creek during the late afternoon, then snaked up into the broken tailings of the Santiago Mountains. The western sky was a thick crimson smear when they topped a ledge and paused, squinting, while their tired horses nuzzled the nape of dried yellow grass at trailside. A harsh desert landscape spread endlessly before them, a rumpled, limestone-tawny blanket folded by cliffs and ridges, pinched by arroyos and canyons, and lined with topaz and sapphire streamers from the setting sun.

One of the riders was a woman. Licking parched lips, Jessica Starbuck heeled her mount forward, anxious to reach their destination and take up the mysterious, tacitly dangerous appeal that had piqued her to come. About mid-twenties, taut-breasted, lithe-hipped, tall and leggy, she had a feline's sensuous way of moving—even when wearily astride a livery stable's ill-fitting saddle. She was clad in a snug cambric shirt, worn denims, a broad brown belt, and riding boots. The sun's slanting rays gleamed off stray wisps of her coppery-blond hair, which she wore softly coiled beneath a flat-crowned, wide-brimmed hat. The sultry warmth extended to her tanned face, with its high cheekbones and audacious green-specked eyes. And yet, at the moment, her features couldn't hide the exhausting, heat-sapping effects of their trek across Texas from her Circle Star Ranch.

Like Jessie, her riding companion was tired. Yet Ki rode upright in his saddle, a man in his early thirties whose lean, sinewy body was graced with energy and agility. Born in Japan to an American sea captain and his Nipponese wife, his father had given Ki his respectable height and natural stamina; while from his mother, he'd inherited his almond-shaped eyes, straight blue-black hair, and that handsome bronze complexion denoting mixed parentage. Orphaned early, forced to survive as a half-breed outcast, Ki had apprenticed himself to one of the last samurai masters and trained in all forms of martial arts. Migrating to California, he was hired by Alex Starbuck, the international business magnate, to guard his daughter Jessie.

So Ki made his home at the Circle Star, here in the Southwest where crossbreeding was too common to draw interest, much less prejudice. And as usual, he wore nondescript range garb—faded jeans, loose-fitting collarless shirt, old black leather vest, and a dusty, stained Stetson whose crown was battered all out of shape. His feet were clad in Asian-style rope-soled cloth slippers, but in this land of moccasins and sandals, even these passed notice. That was fine by him. Those who knew Ki sized him up as calm yet alert by temperament, laconic, and devoted like a brother to Jessie and her farflung interests. As Jessie's

2

companion and confidant since the murder of her father, Ki was, in a sense, the protector behind the throne, and as such he felt more comfortable out of the spotlight.

Well, they were about out of light altogether, Ki opined, scanning the bleak ridges ahead. And that didn't set comfy with him one whit. A gut feeling began to nag him, too, a premonition, or maybe just nerves, but pesky nonetheless.

Riding up alongside Jessie, Ki shifted irritably in his seat and muttered, "We're being watched."

Jessie twisted about, but saw no vestige of life. "Where?"

"In the air, underfoot—damned if I know." He nodded toward the fissured escarpments looming higher and more forbidding. "Where they'd have the drop on us, I reckon, so if we're being watched from anywhere, it'd be from up on one of those slopes."

Jessie nodded, knowing from experience to heed his intuitions. Besides, she was growing uneasy now. As dusk fell softly, quietly, and they continued winding among fissured cliffs and chasms, her hand never strayed far from the Winchester '73 .44 carbine in her saddle scabbard.

This was not the only weapon they carried. A custom Colt revolver was holstered on Jessie's right thigh, and a two-shot derringer was cunningly stashed behind her big brass belt buckle. Ki toted no pistol or gunbelt, but in his vest were secreted short daggers and other small throwing weapons, including a supply of *shuriken*—little, razor-sharp, star-shaped steel disks. As well, he took from his scabbard a Model 76 .50-90 Winchester Express repeater and laid it lengthwise across his lap. He disliked firearms as a rule, but out in the desert, a long-range big-bore rifle was a gratifying edge to hold.

The wagon path faded into deepening murk. The ruggedness of the hemming slopes dulled with encroaching night, blurring over and filling in with shadows. Full darkness smudged the Santiagos further, to a textured ebony as unfathomable as the swarthy sky.

The moon was up by the time Jessie and Ki entered

Persimmon Gap, one of the few passes into the Big Bend country. Yet the moon, a pallid last-quarter crescent, and the sprinkling of stars cast little light, and the depths of Persimmon Gap remained shrouded in gloom. Jessie probed the blackness ahead, an apprehensive sensation chilling her between her shoulder blades, and she kept casting glances now and then along their backtrail. Ki rode with his eyes scrutinizing the corrugated sides pressing close around them—shrouded, silent, menacing.

Something caused his horse's ears to prick nervously.

Ki stiffened and pulled up. Jessie halted, tense and listening. Other than a faint sigh of wind, all was as still as death. . . . They were about to move on when they heard something that might have been the wind, but they doubted it. An almost inaudible featherish sound, like a plant brushing a rock. But not likely. . . .

Nearby, a horse neighed with startling suddenness.

Immediately they neck-reined about, wheeling savagely. At the same instant a rifle cracked, its bullet sizzling by Jessie's ear. The shot was reverberating when a salvo of gunfire blasted from the same area, not far ahead, against the stone walls. The slugs ripped harmlessly wide, Jessie and Ki already veering sharply to the left. A guttural bull-roarer of a voice bellowed out:

"Mi santo puta! Kill the fools!"

Caught off guard, the ambushers recovered and launched after their victims. By then Jessie and Ki were racing for a tumble of boulders along the bank behind them, hoping their tuckered mounts wouldn't give out under them. Glancing back, they saw the gunmen charging in a noisy swarm with their loud-mouthed leader, an ugly brute by any measure, bewhiskered, square-headed, chunky-bodied. An anthill sombrero hung down his back from a strap around his throat, and in his fists bucked a pair of big old Dragoons, adding to the volleys his men were hurling at the fleeing pair.

The boulders loomed nearer, spilling like a rockslide

4

from a notch in the slope behind. But the pursuers were closing faster. Jessie whipped out her pistol for short-range work, triggering into the looming crush. Similarly, Ki twisted around and sent a handful of *shuriken* winging back, the way a gambler would deal a deck of cards. There were howls and screams and jostling confusion, and a few bodies plunged underhoof, but the mob stormed on to engulf them. Shots snapped and whined after them as they bent low over their horses' withers, desperate to hit the boulders before the bullets hit them.

Abruptly Ki straightened, brought his mount to a slewing halt by the rockfall. Taking his rifle, he left the saddle in a leap, spanked his horse bolting out of range, and began laying cover fire for Jessie. He emptied two more saddles as the gunmen, swerving, fanned out along the sides of the pile. By then Jessie reached the shelter of the boulders, diving beside him.

"We're not home free yet," she said, hurriedly reloading. "We're too out in the open here, and they're blocking the trail."

Ki nodded, glancing up the slide to the caved-in notch of the bank. "We've got to move back, up into that cut."

They began a grim, fighting retreat to the slope. Snarling lead chased after them, ricocheting wildly off rock, kicking up gouts of stinging shards. Pressing her cheek against the stock of her carbine, Jessie triggered off a shot and knocked the horse out from under a gunman. He rolled and scrambled into a run, only to be downed when her second round struck him in the chest.

Another rider lunged to pick up the wounded man. His head was burst apart by a high-velocity slug from Ki. Persimmon Gap resounded with crackling gunfire, bloodcurdling cries, and the rataplan of horses, the onslaught raging so ferocious that Ki almost missed the sneak attack. But aware that the gunmen might try to cut them off from the slope, he wasn't surprised when he glimpsed a dark shape behind them, darting in from one boulder to another.

5

Warning, "Watch your back!" Ki left Jessie his rifle and sprang after the man, right hand digging into his vest. Guns were worse than useless, he believed, in places where the walls pressed close.

The gunman believed different. As Ki bore in, dodging and weaving, the man hastily let loose with an old Starr .44 revolver. A bullet whistled past Ki's cheek, its breath hot and vicious so closely did it singe his skin, when he tossed the dagger balanced in his hand. The gunman buckled as the blade sunk into his chest, and then he collapsed among the rocks, face up, arms outstretched, his revolver lying in his open palm.

Three more gunmen broke from covering rocks, scurrying in a zigzaggy rush at Ki. The advancing hail of lead from their weapons forced Ki to flatten. Jessie, tracking them with her carbine, hit the first in the breastbone, the second when he turned, and the third in his lower back when he was fleeing toward the trail. That took some of the steam out of the remaining gunmen, riders slowing, milling, some bickering in Spanish with their leader, gesturing angrily at their dead.

Hustling to take advantage of the respite, Ki retrieved his rifle and started at a run up the slide. Jessie followed. Spotting them, the riders on the trail let out a resurgent yell, and again the caverous Gap reverberated with the thundering blasts of their weapons. As they hunched sprinting for a clump of stone and scrub in the notch, something burned a gash along Jessie's back. An inch lower and she'd have been dead as those three sneaky gunmen, she thought.

They gained the shelter of the clump safely. Their backs were against the bank now, in a black pocket above the gunmen, with escape lying dark and inviting over the slope behind. Bullets searched the slope for them, but they were no longer visible targets. Cursing shouts of consternation and disappointment rose from the gunmen, changing to howls of shock as from the dark niche there burst a volley

6

of rifle-fire. A couple more bit the dust, and another choked with pain as a bullet smashed his arm. Their compadres were not slow in reining their frantic horses and sheering aside.

Blistering the air with Latin invective, their leader tried to rally his faltering crew. Some obeyed, firing wildly at the clump where nothing moved, but from which the deadly fusillade continued to pour. Ki, hunkering alongside Jessie, aimed his rifle at the leader, his onyx eyes gleaming as he squeezed the trigger. He caught the man nearest the leader when the leader zigged and the other man zagged at the last possible instant. The man toppled against the leader's dun stallion, which shied and almost unseated the leader, who hastily slewed his mount about, changing his mind as well as his direction. Ordering his henchmen away, he beat a hasty retreat down the trail before Ki could draw a bead again.

Laying down a final barrage of lead, the surviving gunmen rapidly collected their dead and wounded. Then, with a last defiant howl, they sped furiously after their leader, fading into the shadows as quickly as they had come.

For quite a while Jessie and Ki remained behind the rock barricade. There was no further sign of the gunmen, no sound to indicate that they were near. A silence hung over Persimmon Gap, heavy and ominous.

Jessie shifted restlessly. "You think we should head on out? We'll have to sooner or later."

"Let's make it later," Ki advised. "They might be waiting for just such a move."

Jessie sat down on a large flat rock and sighed. Ki was right; he had taught her the tricks of attacks and fighting, and she knew better than to be caught by leaving cover too soon. Still, she sounded impatient. "Beyond that, I wonder what they're up to, where they plan to go."

"Back across the Rio, judging by their lingo," Ki said. "They struck me as some border-hopping *bandidos*, on the

7

prowl for stray loot, lone travelers, whatever seemed easy to swipe or waylay safely.''

''Well, maybe. But I've a hunch they hid here in ambush expressly for us, not just anybody, to come along.''

Ki frowned quizzically. ''Now, how'd they know who we were and where we'd head? We've told no one.''

''Perhaps we didn't have to. Someone may've learned or guessed beforehand that we're coming, someone who doesn't want Starbuck mixing into things here.''

''I wouldn't doubt it. Even so, Jessie, these *lobos* ain't been waiting around since we left the Circle Star.''

Pausing, Jessie thought back over their journey. She recalled the sleepy *mestizo* at Fort Pena, who had ridden out of the settlement right after he had heard—or rather, could have overheard—a stranger inquire about the Olivers. At the time it had meant nothing to speak of, but now with hindsight, Jessie related the incident to Ki. Assuming a tie-in, though, she still couldn't answer how the ambush was connected with the cryptic telegram that had launched her trip:

ALMACEN'S, FORT PENA SETTLEMENT, 12:35 PM
MISS JESSICA STARBUCK
CIRCLE STAR RANCH, SARAH, TEXAS
FATHER DIED. GOOSE EGG TOO MUCH. SEND YOUR BRO-
KERAGE AGENTS AT ONCE, MUST BE GOOD FIGHTERS AND
ARMED. WILL SUPPLY FACTS, FIGURES, FULL RUN, CLEAR
TITLE, AND NO HAGGLE. KNOW STARBUCK WILL GIVE FAIR
PRICE FOR PROPERTY AND STOCK AS IT COMES.
MISS PRUDENCE OLIVER
MASHED-O, INGOT, TEXAS

On the surface, the message resembled numerous other distressed-sale offers that arrived at Starbuck headquarters. But this one touched Jessie personally, for Prudence Oliver was an old school chum from St. Anne de Beaupre Academy for Damoiselles. Jessie had always liked her spunky, unspoiled nature, and had kept in contact after Pru's father, Hugo Oliver, took her out of school following the death of her mother in childbirth. Now she had no family.

But there was more to it than that.

For starters, Pru was five hundred miles from home. The Mashed-O Ranch, familiarly called the Goose Egg, was named after Hugo Oliver's cattle brand, a wide O. And as long as Jessie had known Pru, the Mashed-O had always been a middlin' spread up in the Nueces country. Ingot, Texas, was not. Jessie couldn't pinpoint Ingot exactly—it was too new or two-bit, apparently, to show on a map yet—but Pru had sent her wire from Fort Pena, which presumably was the nearest telegraph point to Ingot. Fort Pena served as a gateway to the Big Bend country some eighty miles to the south, a lawless, wild, and desolate region, and a helluva far cry from Nueces.

Considering the Big Bend, Pru's advice to send able fighters made sense. To Jessie, it also implied a deeper, more intense threat was focused against the Mashed-O, though perhaps she'd read too much into it. But what had Pru meant by "as it comes"? Probably the phrase *as is*, yet Pru knew her English, so maybe she wrote that on purpose. It was a puzzler; the whole offer was a puzzler, Jessie thought; the urgent rush to dump her family ranchstead didn't sound like the Prudence she remembered.

True, her father's death could've left Pru distraught. Jessie might have chalked it all up to despair, except that Hugo Oliver had been one ornery cuss. Pru had tolerated him out of blood loyalty, but as far as Jessie knew, there'd never been any vast love lost between the two.

So maybe Pru needed to sell, maybe not. Overall, though, Jessie had the impression that she badly needed help, and she must have it at once.

Four days later Jessie and Ki reached Fort Pena by stage. The depot was in the settlement, which had grown up around a subtler's post outside the fort proper. The depot entrance was one doorway in a block-long wall of doorways, all lettered differently, and all leading into the same barn-sized room. The big sign atop the roof of the galleried boardwalk was painted: ALMACEN'S EMPORIUM * NEEDS OF EVERY TRADE, WHIMS OF EVERY NATURE. There was no Mr. Almacen; the name was a bastardization of the Spanish for a shop or warehouse.

The stage arrived in the dead of the afternoon, siesta time. The settlement slumbered, the handful of folks outside moving according to where the shade was. Children, dogs, and goats hung around, brain-fried.

While Ki headed for the livery stable, Jessie stopped by the telegraph office in Almacen's. The interior was cooler and dimmer, but scarcely livelier. A light patronage of ranch hands, laborers, off-duty soldiers, Anglo, Mexican, *mestizo*, and a couple of Indians were settled around the main bar like camels at an oasis. And they smelled about as bad, Jessie thought, what with their sweat, cigars, and unwashed bodies.

She crossed to the telegraph office, which was basically a desk at the corner of the building where the wires fed in, gussied up with a counter and a wicket and a big, bad oil painting of Winged Mercury. The telegrapher was sitting by an open window, fanning himself with his pad of flimsies. Seeing Jessie approach, he struggled to get up, torn between the effort to move and the desire for company. Jessie told him to stay put and moved to the end of the counter, near where he sat. She checked for messages for Starbuck—there were none—and in the course of conversation, casually asked about the Olivers of the Mashed-O, who had sent wires from here from time to time.

Offhand, the telegrapher could not recollect her friends or their ranch. "Too many newcomers to our environs," he declared, but proudly, like a civic booster. "We'll be a reg'lar metropolis, mark my word. There's talk of the Texas and New Orleans railroad a-comin', and an ol' sailor who's here wants to name our town Marathon, 'cause the area reminds him of Marathon, Greece.''

''Sounds promising. Speaking of such, I'm sort of on the lookout for a town named Ingot. I'm given to understand it's somewhere hereabouts.''

''More like thereabouts, I'm afeared. Ingot is way south, almost to the river,'' he said, referring to the Rio Grande. ''It's on the east side of the Rosillos Mountains, just below the slopes where they hit silver a couple of years ago. That sparked a rush, and Ingot took root on the river there. Hey, you ain't harboring notions of traipsing down there, is you?''

''Why? What's wrong with Ingot?''

''Nie to everything, but that ain't it. To the south and east run the Espantosa Hills—that's why.''

''Espantosa,'' Jessie repeated. ''That's Spanish for 'haunted.' You don't aim to tell me that people living down there are scared of haunts?''

''They're plenty scairt of the kind of haunts what hang out in them hills,'' the telegrapher said moodily, and glancing away, stared out the window.

Jessie hesitated. The telegrapher didn't pick up his conversation, but leaned toward the open window, shooing a fly out. Jessie was about to prompt him with a question when suddenly he stuck his head out and yelled.

''I sees yuh! Git! You can't squatter here, drat yuh! Go on, git!''

Jessie heard scuffing sounds and saw a sarape-wrapped *mestizo* rise from a crouch outside the window. Yawning, wavering, the *mestizo* shuffled off as though seeking a more peaceful spot of shade. The telegrapher craned out for a final look, then sat down again—and the telegraph key started clattering.

Jessie left him busily taking a message.

After going outside, she went down to the livery and turned in at the wide dark doors of the stable. Up by Almacen's, the movement of someone out in the sun-

11

bleached, deserted street caught her attention, and she paused for a moment. The sleepy *mestizo* had ambled to the hitchrail and mounted a jaded pinto.

Standing shadowed in the doorway, Jessie watched the *mestizo* dozing in the saddle as the crowbait nag ambled down the street. The *mestizo* paid no attention to anything, head nodding under his wide, shabby sombrero. He disappeared finally on the trail to the south, unhurried and placid.

Jessie rubbed an earlobe thoughtfully and then shrugged. The *mestizo* was probably all he seemed, a sleepy rider from one of the southern ranches who'd visited the Settlement for a chaw and a snort of tequila. She turned from the door and went to join Ki.

Before long they rode back to the stage depot in Almacen's and claimed their personals that had come on the stage. Ki had bought the best bits of horseflesh and gear that Fort Pena had for sale; he rode a deep-brisketed hammerhead roan, while Jessie was astride a steeldust grulla that promised plenty of stamina. They started their long ride south, which would eventually bring them here in the heat-blasted rocks of Persimmon Gap. . . .

Jessie's tired voice sounded from the ground, where she sat on the flat rock. "The eavesdropper, a *mestizo*, and the bandidos were Mexican. Ki, I'm positive their big *jefe* with the cowhorn bellow is directly linked up to his *maracas* with the Mashed-O."

"I'm not so certain, Jessie. You know Pru Oliver better'n I do, but from what I know, she wouldn't take an hombre like that in her confidence. No, I'll bet you a plugged peso that if it turns out to be anyone, it'll be someone close to the ranch."

Jessie said nothing. Ki scanned the ridge above, whose top showed faintly against the starlight. In the shadows Jessie could not read the expression on his face, but it was apparent that he was mulling over ideas, just as she was.

The moon climbed higher and then seemed to dip toward

12

the far canyon wall. Ki stretched, watching the steely glitterings of the stars, then turned to Jessie. "Cover me. I'm going to take a *pasear* outside."

Jessie came quickly to her feet and Ki slipped down through the rocks, out into the open trail of the Gap. He crouched there a moment, fingers hooked in the pockets of his vest. There was no blast of gunfire. Cautiously he started along the trail in the direction their horses had gone, studying the surroundings carefully. Nothing stirred along the trail or steep banks. Only the slopes and ridges, an immense inanimateness, appeared in his gaze. It almost made a guy believe those bastards had vamoosed.

He didn't have to hike far to find their mounts. Although capable and energetic, the horses had the imperturbable disposition of most livery stock, docile and disinclined to wander freely when left on their own. Ki caught them slowly dragging their reins as they cropped on the scant grass along the trail. Jessie left the cover of the slope when Ki returned with the mounts, feeling a sense of relief as she swung into saddle.

They rode on warily through Persimmon Gap, alert and ready for trouble, checking their backtrail often. They half-expected bullets to crash into them, and they were almost surprised when none did.

★

Chapter 2

The balance of their journey to Ingot proved uneventful.

Located on the bank of a mountain stream, the mining town owed its existence to an ore-reducing stamp mill, which required a plentiful water supply. Saloons, gaming dens, and whorecribs clustered along its busy main street with false-framed shops and storefronts, while higher up the rough slopes spread a haphazard rash of miners' tents and hovels. And throughout it pervaded the monotonous rumble of the mill, as huge iron pestles ground ore to a watery paste from which silver would be extracted by the amalgam process.

"I've seen rawer camps," Ki observed, "but rarely."

"I could do with never seeing it again," Jessie added, glancing around. "Looks like that silver strike attracted all sorts of hombres, all itching for diversion and not particular about the brand, so long as it made for excitement."

Ki chuckled. But a moment later, as they ambled leisurely along the main street, he lost his humor. Without warning a gunshot cracked thunderously and a bullet turned Jessie's hat sideways on her head. Immediately they dropped from their saddles, reaching for weapons as they landed lightly on their feet.

The next instant they realized that the bullet had not been meant for Jessie. Down the street galloped a big bay horse. Leaning low in the saddle to present as small a target as possible, a hatless, coatless man was spurring his mount to greater speed. After him raced a man on foot, a man whose face streamed with blood and who held a smoking rifle.

Just as the running man came abreast of Jessie and Ki, he halted, flung the rifle to his shoulder and sent another slug whining after the rider. The rider swerved unhurt around the last building on the street and vanished southward in a cloud of dust.

The rifleman grounded his long gun, cussed bitterly, and mopped his bloody face with a bandanna. "Sorry, ma'am," he called to Jessie. "Reckon that shot of mine sidled a mite close to you. Some dadburn blood got into my eyes and throwed me off."

Jessie removed her hat and tentatively fingered the bullet hole in the crown. "I'm glad you pulled high," she noted dryly. "You might learn to squeeze a trigger instead of jerking on it, though."

"What's this all about?" Ki demanded, showing a little hard iron in his voice. "Is potshooting folks some kind of afternoon pastime in Ingot?"

"The sneaky polecat was cold-decking a game in my place," the man replied. He swabbed at the blood, which they now saw came from an ugly gash just above his left brow. "When I caught him, he bent a gun barrel over my noggin and skedaddled. I grabbed a rifle and took chase, and if it ain't been for blood messing my aim, he'd be sporting horns and a pitchfork right now." The man bound the kerchief about his head, wincing, then gestured toward

16

a building a short ways up the street. "That's my joint, run respectable and accommodating ladies. C'mon in for a snor—eh, a beverage on the house, to even up for ventilating your topper, ma'am. Your horses and gear will be safe at the tierack across the street. I got a lookout settin' by the window with a sawed-off, keeping an eye on the patrons' mounts."

Quickly Jessie and Ki hitched their horses, loosened saddle girths, and followed the man through a gathering crowd into his establishment. It was a clapboard structure festooned with gingerbread and gimcrackcry, a batwing entrance at one end and a frosted-glass door at the other. A painted wooden sign above the batwings read PAYDIRT BAR; scrolling etched in the frosted glass read PARLOR.

The man ushered them in the parlor door. Inside was a spartan lounge, its only decor other than the requisite tables and chairs being a poorly stuffed bison head. There was a sprinkling of women present, chatting together or socializing with male escorts; whether they were *ladies*, Jessie thought, appeared questionable.

Although a common wall divided the parlor from the Paydirt Bar, much of the span was an open archway. Filling the saloon were burly miners, laborers, and ranchhands, along with a number of bleach-eyed jaspers tight of mouth and long of twist, who didn't look like they lived by twirling a rope or busting rocks. A long carved-oak bar was lined with drinkers, several poker games were in play, and chuck-a-luck and roulette tables were operating. Raucous noise eddied through the archway; Jessie and Ki heard the harsh roar of talk and laughter, the clink of glasses and bottles, then the horrawin' welcome of their host.

"The jackleg got away," the man answered the volley of questions. "Last I seen him, he was foggin' for the Espantosas like the devil beatin' tanbark. Okay! Okay! F'get it. But the next tinhorn can bet on gettin' plugged first and told about it afterwards."

17

"That's the way to talk, Gotch-ear!" a miner shouted. "The Paydirt is notorious for square dealin'! Keep 'er straight!"

Jessie and Ki had already noted that the man had a notched ear, presumably sliced by a passing bullet in the course of some ancient row. Sitting down now at one of the tables, they introduced themselves and learned that his last name was Gillespie. The aptly monikered Gotch-ear was squat, broad, with pendulous arms and hands, and feet like a puncher's warbag laid out flat. His nose had been broken and carelessly set. His hair was carroty-red and bristly. With the blood-soaked bandanna tied around his head, and his wide mouth grin-quirked at the corners, Gotch-ear Gillespie resembled a truculent but cheerful pirate.

"Name your ruin," he offered heartily as a bartender hustled in from the saloon carrying a bottle and glassware. "Whiskey, my private stock, for me and this gent, Sam," he instructed the bartender, without waiting for Ki to reply. "Nothing but the best for my guests. I owe Miss Starbuck here a new hat for hers I drilled—wish it'd been that cardsharper's hide instead—and they've agreed to square it up in drink." Then turning to Jessie, Gotch-ear suggested, "Perhaps you'd fancy a glass of female tonic. Seems to be quite popular with the ladies."

"No doubt, but no thanks." She smiled modestly. "A little brandy might be nice, though."

"Just as wise," Gotch-ear conceded. "I sampled some tonic once. It's akin to stump blasting powder, about a hundred and ten proof, I'd hazard. Can't no man handle it."

"If these folks swallow a hat's worth of this popskull hooch, they'll wish you'd aimed a foot lower," Sam asserted, a lanky, melancholic-faced man with one eye that focused in one direction and the other one in another.

"Sam's sore," Gotch-ear countered as the bartender poured two glasses. "He used to be a lookout, but the customers said nobody could tell who in blazes he was

18

looking at. One time he threw down on a rowdy at the bar, and everyone in the back of the house went under tables. So I had to put him to tending bar. Nobody minds a cross-eyed bartender.''

"I wasn't cross-eyed till I made a mistake and took a drink in here,'' Sam retorted. ''Innocent strangers smellin' a cork out of one of Gotch-ear's bottles have been crippled for life.'' Setting the bottle down, he said to Jessie, ''I'll see if I can find any decent brandy around, but don't count on it,'' and hastened off to wait on the thirsty bar patrons.

Gotch-ear huffed indignantly. ''Confound his wretched insolence, I ought to . . . ! Don't know why I haven't! Well, Sam had better fetch you your brandy, Miss Starbuck, and pronto, else this time I f'certain will!''

Jessie ignored the unspecified threat, doubting Gotch-ear ever had one in mind. He and Sam must've been mudslinging for years, patently for their own amusement, though they'd be too stubborn to admit it. ''Please, don't bother about the brandy,'' she said. ''Thanks all the same, but we gather we've got a far piece to go yet, and we really should be moving on.''

''You gather? Strangers hereabouts, eh?'' Gotch-ear took the bait, hooking his curiosity. ''Folks, I don't mean to be prying personal. Tell me to go tend my own baliwick. But y'see, hereabouts *is* my baliwick, so if you're a mind to, I can give ways and means to wherever you're heading.''

''Much obliged.'' Jessie was a mind to. After the ambush, though, she was not about to trust Ingot, asking blindly for directions. Nor was she taking Gotch-ear on faith, but at least she'd had a few minutes to size him up and take him on a gamble. ''We're looking for the Mashed-O.''

''Why, that spread's to the south, down in Mooneye Valley.''

''Odd name for a place,'' Ki remarked.

''Actually, it's pretty befitting. A mooneye, remember, is when you've got moon- or night-blindness and can't see

19

but poorly in the dark. Well, Mooneye Valley has seen many herds drive through it, mostly at night, in blind dark,'' Gotch-ear explained, and advised them as to the best route. "Problem is, the valley runs next to the Espantosa Hills. There're trails through those hills that lead down to Mexico by about the shortest course hereabouts. The rustlers use 'em. They've been using 'em for years to sift wet cows over the Rio, both coming and going. And before that, the Apaches crossed the river and rode 'em on their way to raids in the north. Hiding out in them hills now are renegades and owlhoots who shoot on sight, when they ain't cahootin' across the border at Quevidas, a little Mexican rathole. The whole snakefest of 'em act dead set against neighbors close to the hills. It might sort of cramp their style, I reckon, but anyhow they've struck everyone trying to make a go of that range. Hugo Oliver knew it, too. I recollect him getting warned of trouble, when he was wanting to start ranching down there.''

Jessie leaned forward. "Warned? Who's threatened him?''

"No, no threat. Oliver was forewarned, I mean, cautioned by the owner of the land, Zed Rykoff, even before Zed agreed to sell. Zed didn't need the land, but kept control in case neighbors of the wrong sort should take a notion to squat there. Since he didn't work it, he didn't tangle much with outlaws, but he told Oliver about all the trouble, including what befell the two buyers before him. Oliver didn't scare. Said he wasn't hunting cover for no trouble. Well, he didn't get trouble. They murdered him before he could have any.''

"We had word that Hugo Oliver was dead, but not that he was killed," Jessie said slowly, somberly. "How . . . how did it happen?''

"Fast. Oliver had barely taken possession and moved into the ranchhouse. His trail herd hadn't even arrived here yet, and I suspect much of his crew was away driving it, putting him short-handed. Easier to catch out. Someone blew off the lower half of his face, with what appears to've been a muzzle-loading shotgun filled with birdshot and horseshoe nails. That sort of thing leaves a distinctive mark. What with his death, and with his herd showing up a couple of days ago, his daughter inherited enough trouble to sink her up to her ears.''

Gotch-ear downed his drink and reached for the bottle to pour another. Jessie looked shaken, and revolted. Poker-faced, Ki watched Gotch-ear and decided he believed him, kind of liked him, even. Before anything more could be said, a hubbub erupted in the barroom near the batwing entrance. It was a fairly tame outburst as saloon commotions go, but it was enough to draw their attention.

The clamor seemed to be centered on three men entering the bar. One was a muscle-bound pugugly in his mid-thirties, his face rubbery and unshaven, with loose corrupt lips and truculent eyes. About his same age or possibly a little older, a second man was slender and well set up, with a handsome tanned face that seemed to wear a perpetual smile, and eyes as cold as well chain that seemed to call his mouth a liar. The third was younger, late-twenties, with a husky build somewhere between the other two, clad in linsey-woolsey shirt and butternut pants and wearing a cartridge bandolier across his muscular chest. His companions wore corduroy and cotton, and they all wore heavy, flat-soled laced boots.

The two older men took seats at a table, which chanced to be within easy view of the parlor archway. They were not the cause of the hullabaloo. The third man was angry at the top of his voice, and apparently some of the miners were not exactly ecstatic about him. From batwings to archway, the man loudly wrangled with as many as cared to match lungs, and then he came stalking into the parlor. His battered hat was tipped over one glittering brown eye, and his devil-take-the-hindmost bearing caused Jessie to associate him with ruckus raising in general.

Gotch-ear groaned. ''Lawdalmighty, it's Wade Duval. Here comes trouble.''

"You hear 'em, Gotch-ear? You hear 'em?" Duval yelled as he approached, waving a hand back toward the barroom. "Miners are threatening to desert, and after that raid last week, when Oglethorpe got shot dead and three others got winged, I goddamn well can't blame 'em if they hightail for hellangawn."

"Easy, Wade, ladies are present," Gotch-ear chided, trying to derail him. Immediately he launched into making introductions, informing Jessie and Ki, "Y'see, Wade is the office manager for the Fortuna Mine, up in the slopes. He handles the payroll and the hefty sums of cash to pay off the miners."

"Exactly why I'm here," Duval declared, back on track. "I've got to have your help, God help me. The coming payroll is a whopper, biggest yet, surely a target. I need your Regulators to guard the safe round the clock till payday."

"Wade, you know better'n such," Gotch-ear said. "We're just townsfolk who go help each other as need arises. To do what you want, why, we'd have to neglect our businesses and leave Ingot wide open. That's the whole point for us getting together."

"If anything happens to the payroll, you can kiss your point good-bye," Duval contended. "The miners can't get far before payday, and afterward won't get farther'n Ingot, I bet. But if they're not paid, every manjack will bolt."

Gotch-ear shrugged. "If it's so important, let them guard it."

"Oh, yeah. Talk about foxes guarding the chicken coop. And them's that ain't foxes ain't fighters, either. Plus they'd have to be paid, and so would their replacements doing their mining. That, as Big Nick says, is horsecocky."

There was a short, nasty silence.

Jessie spoke up. "Mr. Duval, what kind is your safe?"

"Eh? Oh, it's an Acme, the Leviathan model."

"Combination, double doors, forty-eight square feet, and weighs a ton," Jessie recalled, eyeing Duval. Up

22

close, she judged him to be six feet one or two, maybe two hundred pounds, with a hardness that didn't come from riding a brass rail. Tousled hair the shade of dressed harness leather, brushed long under that rakish hat. Big beak of a nose and an anvil for a chin. Eyes of merry sinning that appraised her squarely. A holstered Remington .44-40 on his belt, an old model, showing much use but also much care. This was no wild hotspur, despite his display of temper; he was a man used to giving orders and having them obeyed. She liked him immediately.

But she didn't pull any punches. "I know Acmes, all right. How long will your payroll be kept in that sardine can of a safe, Mr. Duval?"

Taken aback, suspicious lights flared in Duval's eyes, then dimmed as he gave Jessie another long appreciative study. "Payday's a week from tomorrow."

"And making for general deviltry," Gotch-ear deplored.

"Don't cry me no tears, you ol' crocodile," Duval snapped, and turned back to Jessie. "Why do you want to know?"

"Because guards aren't going to save you. Post them ten-deep around the safe, and a diversion, a fire, explosion, any number of things could empty the place. If I were you, I'd take precautions against having your safe blown open one of these nights by some burglar."

"Would you, now. Like what?"

"Depends. The mine has a store of blasting powder, hasn't it?"

Duval nodded. "So you want to blow the safe before they do, right?"

"No, I'd fill the extra space in the safe with powder," Jessie said, "and hang a label beside the combination dial explaining what you'd done. Now, a thief might think you were bluffing—but if he *did* blast the safe, he'd probably get killed trying it. And at least the payroll money wouldn't fall into his hands. It would be blown to shreds."

A grin broke over Wade Duval's face. "Ma'am, I'll do

just that. I have to 'fess I've never thought much of that safe. Safes have to be toted by muleback into the mountains, so we couldn't get a better-built, larger-sized vault for storing the Fortuna's funds. Well, I should go check how Leo and Big Nick are faring, I guess." He shook hands with Ki and Gotch-ear, then tipped his hat to Jessie, saying, "I'm sure glad to've met you, Miss Starbuck. Hope to see you again real soon."

Gotch-ear stared agape as Duval strutted back into the saloon. "I never anticipated to see the day when that catamount gentled down to a tabby."

"Maybe he's feeling sickly," Ki suggested deadpan. "Possibly an onset of noxia or flux, or p'raps dropsy, hydrangia, or paralytic dementia."

"Egad! I hope whatever they is, they ain't contagious!"

"Who're the men with him?" Jessie hurriedly asked Gotch-ear, giving Ki a look fit to maim. "I believe Mr. Duval called them Leo and Big Nick."

"Yes'm. The big feller is Big Nick Tualatin. He owns the Fortuna, struck the claim about two years ago. The other gent is Leo Frost, Big Nick's mine superintendent. Leo is a nice feller, never saying a word out of turn, always quiet and polite. Big Nick is just the opposite. He's foul tempered and a bully, and gets ugly when he drinks. Gambles a lot and is always beefin' and argufyin' with the other players."

"He looks handy with his fists, okay," Ki remarked.

"Big Nick's a mauler. But don't see Leo Frost short. T'uther night Big Nick got quarreling in a poker game. The cuss across the table pulled a knife, and I reckon if Leo hadn't grabbed his wrist quick as lightning, the knifer would've cut Big Nick to tatters. Likely died doing it, too." Gotch-ear paused to take a drink, then reflected: "Leo is almighty strong for a slight feller. He nigh broke that gent's wrist when he clamped down, and you could hear the screams at t'uther end of the street. Squeezed all the fight out of the gent. Then Leo said a word to Big Nick and he cooled down pronto. Didn't hear much uproar out of him all evening. He sort of listens to Leo. Don't want to lose him, I reckon. They say he's a mighty fine minin' man."

The slender, smiling Leo Frost glanced over at that moment, as if aware that he was being talked about. He struck a match and fired a cigarette. Ki, suddenly intrigued, watched the lighting with rapt attention.

As Frost turned back, Ki asked, "Where'd they hail from?"

"Wade's out of Amarillo. Learned his trade in the smelters up there. Big Nick and Leo are from New Mexico, I've heard." Gotch-ear scratched his chin. "Uh-huh, both of 'em born and reared in the minin' country over there. They sure know their business."

Jessie nodded. "Their business looks to pack some weight around here. I'm surprised it's not joined your Regulators. Is the mine too far out of town?"

"Yep, too far. Worse, it ain't far enough out. The Fortuna's why we've banded together. Silver brung the miners, built the mill, started the boom. Townfolk had to eat, and them miners craved meat and whiskey. Gents freighted in the redeye, others like Hugo Oliver moved in figuring to supply the beef. Not bad, if it weren't for them outlaws in the Espantosa Hill. The town boomin' and strangers flockin' meant dinero for 'em. They've been wide-looping mighty free, till ranchers are claiming they've more cows south around Quevidas than around here. Replacing the cows, salty curs and border lice have been swarming in. Worsenin' all the time. So we formed the Regulators, but hey, we ain't vigilantes. We're just local shopkeepers trying to hold down the fort, and if it ain't purely legal, it's the closest to law there is hereabouts."

Shortly afterward, Jessie and Ki departed by the parlor door, leaving Gotch-ear heading to his office on the barroom side. They mounted and rode to the livery stable that Gotch-ear had said was down around the next corner.

"It's a clean place and your nags will be safe there," Gotch-ear had told them. "You can get rooms there, too, over the stalls, if you hanker to sleep close to your horses, like some waddies do."

They found the stable satisfactory, but passed on Gotch-ear's suggestion for sleeping accommodations. "No horse ever wanted to sleep near me," Jessie humphed as they left. "And I've no intention of encouraging the notion."

Following the hostler's directions to Ingot's only hotel, they trooped back up the street, past the Paydirt Bar. Beyond stretched a series of smaller storefronts, set close together with only a few alleys leading back to the rear and side lanes. The storefront beside the Paydirt was set so close that it was attached to the side of the building like an addition.

Through the store window, they saw a small, stuffy office, with Gotch-ear seated at a battered, flattop desk. He looked up from the mass of papers on his desk, giving a friendly wave as they went by. Smiling in response, Jessie speculated that the back of the store would be Gotch-ear's private quarters, with a connecting doorway through a side entrance of the building.

Wending their way along the crowded, trash-littered street, they presently wound up at a doorway to a falsefront inscribed, quite arrogantly, GREAT SOUTHWESTERN CONTINENTAL HOTEL. On entering, they discovered that the Great Southwestern Continental boasted a grand total of six rooms, all cubbyholes. And only a single vacancy.

They might have shared one room, except that the bed was akin to a cot, and the formidable proprietress would hear of no such thing. Jessie took the room. From there they walked to a nearby canvas-roofed restaurant. The food proved to be a good-news/bad-news proposition, the bad news being that it was terrible, the good news being there was plenty of it.

The sun had already been touching the crests of the western hills when they had left the Paydirt Bar. It was full dark when they pushed back their chairs in the restaurant and sought the outside once more. Exhausted from their grueling ride, especially that last nie-sleepless push from Persimmon Gap, and believing nothing more could be done before morning, Ki started back to the livery for a room, while Jessie returned to the hotel, wondering if Ki wasn't getting the better of the deal.

Ki passed the series of storefronts, most of them closed for the night, and approached the Paydirt with its adjoining storefront office. There was a light on in Gotch-ear's office, he noticed. His rope-soled slippers made no noise moving through the soft dust filming the boardwalk. He was coming abreast of the office window, when a shot sounded from inside the room. Next door, a pianist had been fumbling idly on the keys in the Paydirt—the music stopped on a discord.

Leaping for the storefront, ready with *shurikens* and daggers, Ki thrust open the entrance door. Gotch-ear was sitting at his desk, his face down on the desktop, arms sprawled. On the outer sidewall, the side opposite the Paydirt, the glass in the window was shattered and tiny wisps of powdersmoke drifted through the opening made by the bullet.

In three bounding steps Ki rounded the corner of the storefront and headed into the narrow alley separating it from the next storefront. Only a few seconds had elapsed since that shot, and the killer had not had time to make much of an escape. Ki spotted him less than five yards from the tiny alley window, a shadowy figure in the darkness.

The man, glancing back, saw Ki and spun around. Ki flattened against the wall, dagger poised in his grasp, as orange flame darted from the muzzle of the man's gun. Ki threw the one dagger, than another at the flare of the gun. His man turned and started to run, but he only took two steps before pitching on his face.

Another gun opened up from the far end of the alley, the

echoes crashing against the close-set walls. Ki felt the breath of one slug just before he jumped around the corner. Without wasting a fraction of a second, he raced past the open door of Gotch-ear's office, ran twenty yards to the corner and then sprinted down the next lane.

Just as he reached the mouth of this alley a dim figure raced by, less than two yards from him. Seeing Ki, he cursed breathlessly and leaped back. Ki saw the moonlight reflect on the muzzle of the gun in his hand. Remembering Gotch-ear sprawled lifelessly over his desk, Ki whipped out his *tanto*, a very short, delicately curved sword—no bigger than a knife, really—from a sheath at the waistband of his trousers. He slashed coolly, coldly, getting his first swipe in before the other went into action. A slug tore his sleeve, nicking his arm, but the triggering had been reflex. Thrusting close and sliding his *tanto* into the man's belly, Ki gutted him up through his chest cavity. He withdrew the knife, quickly wiping its blade clean on the man's shirt, as the gunman collapsed in a gory heap.

Then replacing his *tanto* in its scabbard, Ki ran back to the main street and entered the door of Gotch-ear's office. He saw heads poking out of saloon doors, and several men were hastening from the Paydirt and along the street. Gotch-ear's right side was red with blood. Reluctant to move him any more than was absolutely necessary, Ki swept the desktop clear of papers and stretched him out flat. He said quietly to one of the miners looking through the doorway, "See if you can get a doctor."

He cut away Gotch-ear's shirt and saw the bullet hole in his side. The bar owner was still breathing, and once his eyes flickered open. Blood was trickling from the wound, and Ki stemmed it temporarily with the bandanna from Gotch-ear's head. He studied the spot where the bullet had come out on the other side and then, looking at the smashed window in the alley, his eyes were very hard.

When the doctor broke through the bystanders at the

door, Ki sat off to one side and watched him work on the wound. Somebody had brought in a basin of warm water.

"You'll need a woman to sit with him tonight," the doctor said. "Know anybody?"

Ki shook his head. He looked at the men clustering around the doorway, recognizing Sam the bartender among them, and then one of the others spoke up, "My wife will come over, Doc."

"Can we take him to his room?" Sam asked.

"Soon as I patch him up," the doctor growled testily. "That'll take a lot longer with y'all disrupting me. He's damned lucky that slug wasn't an inch higher. Move along now, let me work in peace."

Ki stood up and walked outside. Sam fell in step, and they went around the corner and down the alley, where several men had discovered the body there. A lantern had been lighted, and Fargo identified the dead man as the rider Gotch-ear had chased.

"Twin skewered," a man said, eyeing the daggers. "Dead as hell."

Sam went with Ki to the other body, whose grisly appearance had attracted a larger crowd. Shouldering through to the front, they studied the rawboned dead man, his broad fleshy nose and glazed black eyes. Nobody in the crowd seemed to know for certain who he was, nor to be at all sure as to just what had happened. Ki did not see fit to enlighten them, here or at the other body.

Heading back, Sam glanced keenly at Ki from his mismated eyes and apparently was satisfied with what he saw. "Mister," he said profoundly, "I've an idea these two hellions were Espantosa Riders."

"What d'you mean?"

"Well, it's on account of goings-on earlier, when Gotch-ear took after the first one for double-dealin'. A pair o' toughs suddenly left their drinks on the bar and hotfooted for the door. But Curtis, the window lookout, blocked 'em with both barrels of his sawed-off cocked, saying nobody was to leave till Gotch-ear returned. Me and the other bartender had ahold of shotguns, too, so they thunk better of it and went back to their drinks. They were gone out the door, though, the instant Gotch-ear came in with you folks.''

"That doesn't make them anything, except curious, maybe. Why'd you call them Espantosa Riders?''

" 'Cause they didn't act like no rubber-neckers who're just curious. They acted like they aimed to cut in. That's the way the Riders do, y'know, sifting into a place by ones and fews, never divulging they know each other, but always ready to gang together at the right time. That's how they're able to heist Fat Annie's saloon last month. When they struck, they was posted all around, so no matter where the crowd turned it was under gun. It's that kind of way the pair was acting like this afternoon,'' Sam insisted, ''like they're sidekicks of the cheat Gotch-ear was after. They must've been. One of 'em is the second dead man we just seen, the body who's gutted like a beef carcass.''

"Sam, you might have something there,'' Ki said thoughtfully. "It's worth considering, anyhow.''

"It's worth clamming up about,'' Sam cautioned as they reached the crowded main street again. "Afraid I've got to get back on the job now. If you see Gotch-ear, tell him I'll drop in on him later.''

As Sam headed for the Paydirt, Ki shouldered through the bystanders to the storefront. Gotch-ear was no longer lying on his desk, but Jessie was standing just inside the entrance, appearing distressed and a mite disheveled.

"I came soon's I heard,'' she said. "The doctor's put Gotch-ear to bed in the back. What's happened?''

"Can't really say,'' Ki replied. "Yet.''

They went into Gotch-ear's living quarters at the rear. The doctor was still there, and a middle-aged woman who was to sit with Gotch-ear. Ki brought a chair over for Jessie and stood looking at Gotch-ear, who was conscious now, stretched out on an iron post bed, his face white and drawn.

Gotch-ear muttered, "Who shot me, Ki?"

"They won't shoot you again. Don't worry about it."

Ki waited until the doctor finished with Gotch-ear and left. He spoke a low word to the woman, and she stepped out for a few moments. Then Ki gave a brisk account of the events, and repeated Sam's conjectures about the pair in the bar.

Gotch-ear swore weakly. "That's what comes of having eyes that look two ways at once. I reckon nothing goes on around the Paydirt that Sam don't see."

"Who are the Espantosa Riders?" Ki asked.

"They're supposed to be an owlhoot outfit which roosts in the Espantosas. They're supposed to be responsible for most of the things what's been happening in this section. I dunno, but it's sure true there's been a heap of organized deviltry hereabouts for the past half year or so. And lots of folks believe in 'em, and believe that anyone who has trouble with 'em might just as well stake a claim in Boot Hill. El Cascabel is claimed to lead 'em."

"El Cascabel? The rattlesnake?"

"Yes'm, that's what he's called," Gotch-ear answered Jessie. "He used to start revolutions below the border, but a couple of years ago the Federalistas finally ran him down and busted up his 'army.' El Cascabel got away, sunk out of sight. When folks got to talking about the Riders, it wasn't long before somebody was saying El Cascabel had organized the gang. Maybe they're right."

"A Mexican?"

"Nope, he ain't Mexican. From this side of the Line, I understand. You hear all sorts of yarns as to what he looks like, but all of 'em agree he's plenty savvy and meaner'n a sore-headed hound. As for him bossing the Riders, if there is such a bunch, the chances are that's just a load of jabber."

"Still, there's no denying the man you chased and the

two Sam reported were together, willing to kill together," Ki said with a frown. "It goes to show the shooting was no spur of the moment impulse. They'd kept tabs on you and knew you worked evenings here, open to the alley window. They knew they could stay off in the dark and fire at you against the light from inside."

Gotch-ear shivered glumly. "Yep, I guess that's the gospel. And listen, you two, because of what you did for me, the pards of them back-shooters are liable to have an eye out for you, too. Your best bet is forget the Mashed-O and hightail out of this gawdforsaken country. That's my advice."

"We appreciate it," Jessie replied, "but won't take it."

"Had a notion you wouldn't," Gotch-ear admitted. "You're loco not to."

"Could be," Jessie said, nodding. "I've observed that once people start running, they usually keep on running for the rest of their lives. Ki is much too lazy and I don't like to run."

★

Chapter 3

Leaving at sunrise, Jessie and Ki headed south out of Ingot as the crimson dawn evolved into another white-hot morning. After some miles the trail forked, the right branch sidling along Tornillo Creek, the left veering off into the broken country to the east. They turned left. Riding easily, camping out in the shade of some cottonwoods during the heat of the day, they traversed the stony desert, through thorny chaparral, over craggy hills.

Late in the afternoon they topped a rise and came to a second forking. The main track continued in the direction of the Dead Horse Mountains. The branch dipped sharply down the sag for several miles and entered the mouth of a valley—Mooneye Valley, Jessie reckoned, according to Gotch-ear's directions. The branch trail, which they followed, then wound on for many more miles through the wide valley between walls of growth-covered hills.

Emerald and amber light glowed above the mountainous

Big Bend vistas when, at dusk, they sighted the Mashed-O ranchhouse. They were yet some distance away when the door opened and a man stepped out. He caught a glimpse of the approaching riders, turned without haste, and stepped back inside the doorway. Jessie exchanged a knowing smile with Ki. The man was taking no chances, prepared to close and barricade the door in an instant, his action seeming typical of this wild and lawless country.

Set in a grove of live oaks, the ranchhouse was a rambling structure of adobe and stone. They rode into the yard and reined up, spotting along one side a circular stone well, the pole fence of a corral, and a combination stable and barn. A few hands hovered about, curious but seemingly unalarmed. The man still remained inside the doorway, a thick-set silhouette, his shadowed eyes level, narrowed as he studied the new arrivals.

"Howdy." He spoke without inflection.

"Is this the Mashed-O?" Jessie asked amicably. "I'm Jessica Starbuck, and my friend here is Ki. We've come to see Prudence Oliver, by invitation."

The man hesitated. Then the tension left him and he stepped out into the yard. "Vaughn Yarbrough, Mashed-O *segundo*. Miz Oliver is busy gussyin' up for supper right now. Light down and feed—chuck's nigh on the table."

Yarbrough hollared for a wrangler to look after their mounts, then ushered them inside. At the end of the hall could be seen the kitchen, where a fat and wrinkled Mexican woman was cooking food at the stove. Glancing in, he told her, "Two more plates, Chita."

Then, as Yarbrough turned to lead the way into the dining room, a young woman entered from a side corridor. Gasping with surprised delight, she cried, "Jessie! And Ki—my heavens!"

Petite, nubile, Prudence Oliver could not have weighed over a hundred and ten pounds soaking wet. Within a year of Jessie's age, she had a piquant face with hazel eyes, a snub nose, and a creamy tanned complexion. Luxuriant auburn hair swathed her head in great looping coils, and the colorful Indian-print dress she wore had leg-o'-mutton sleeves and a belted waist which accentuated the slimness of her figure.

"I'm thrilled to see you both," Pru said, giving them hugs of eager welcome. "But Jessie, at most I expected one of your agents to call on me. What on earth are you doing here?"

"Making up for a long overdue visit. Why, it's been a good three years since we spent Easter together at the Circle Star," Jessie said, sympathizing, "We were deeply grieved by the news of your father's passing."

"No sadder than the loss of your dad, Jessie," Pru replied, heavy-hearted, then forced a smile. "Oh, have you met my cousin?" she asked, introducing Yarbrough. "Second cousin, actually, and ranch foreman."

Yarbrough said, "Howdy," again. In the light he appeared thirtyish, of stocky build and sloping shoulders, wearing a faded plaid shirt and twill pants stuffed into boot-tops. His thick sandy hair hung just a mite long, and his face was narrow with high cheekbones and a pointed, cleft chin. His eyes were muddy, as nearly expressionless as his reserved manner. In fact, the only interest Jessie saw him take was in his cousin.

Chita called in Spanish, and Prudence escorted them into the pleasantly furnished dining room. And though Pru apologized—"It's not fancy, I fear"—the table fairly groaned under platters of meat, potatoes, bread, vegetables, fruits, and drinks. As they sat down, she inquired, "Tell me, Jessie, how was your trip here?"

"A breeze compared to your stunning move from the Nueces," Jessie hedged, preferring not to reveal all that had occurred just yet. "That's what I want to hear about. Your telegram left much to the imagination, you must admit."

"It's quite simple, really. Our region faced another drought like last year, with dry waterholes, windmills

35

pumping air, and the Nueces caked mud for miles at a stretch. Dad felt if we stayed, we'd go bust. Vaughn had already, joining up with us after losing his ranch. He recalled good grazing lands in these parts, from a ride-through years back, before any outlaw squatters,'' Pru explained, a trifle acerbic. "So they went to check around, and Dad found this spread.''

"Hugo thought coming here was a great idea,'' Yarbrough said defensively. "He weren't scairt of outlaws, and didn't reckon there was anything else to be scairt of. Least he didn't have to be leery of roastin' alive without enough water to baste a body proper and keep from burnin' to cracklin's, and I figure that's something.''

Pru sighed. "In any case, we came ahead with a few hands to get things set up, while the crew drove our herd and stuff across half of Texas. The cows grew rackabone, and plenty were lost on the way. Worse, we lost two tophands and our old foreman, Rye Flynn, who was crushed to death when his horse fell on him.'' She lifted her hands in a forlorn shrug. "And Dad, we lost Dad, too.''

Jessie nodded silently, thinking: It's killing her. She could tell how valiantly Pru was meeting the tragedy which had stricken her life, yet how it was becoming too much for her, dragging her down in dismay.

"Too many losses, Jessie. I can't sell you this place.''

"I see,'' Jessie said, seeing nothing. "What're your plans?''

"Hang on, maybe, or deed it back. I'm unsure. Initially I thought you'd take over, wipe out the outlaws, be my revenge. I knew Starbuck had the means, the power to. I forgot it'd still need a crew living here. Whoever I sold to, I'd be causing someone, perhaps a family, to suffer losses like mine, or worse. My conscience would never rest, Jessie. I'm sorry your trip was for nothing.''

"Don't be silly. If all I wanted was to buy you out, I'd have sent a buyer,'' Jessie replied. "Now, let's not discuss it further.''

36

Gladly agreeing, Prudence called Chita to prepare guest rooms. They retired to the parlor and spent the n hours mainly talking, listening, and enjoying a decanter wine. That is, the women talked, Ki mainly listened, and Yarbrough enjoyed the wine.

Eventually the evening drew to a close. Yarbrough bid g'night, and was starting to leave for the bunkhouse when Prudence spoke up, suggesting, "Let's go riding around a bit tomorrow. I haven't seen everything myself; been too busy getting things shaped up. If we head out right after breakfast, there'll be three or four hours before the morning turns hot."

"Sounds fine by me," Jessie said. "From what we saw coming in, it looks like nice holdings, a pretty piece of range."

"Barring the outlaws," Yarbrough growled on his way out. "To blazes with them owlhooters!"

Pru then showed Jessie and Ki to their rooms, where their travelin' bags had been brought earlier. Both had windows overlooking a dark-shadowed outdoor patio and were similarly furnished with a comfortable bunk, a washstand with china bowl and pitcher, an oil lamp, and a tall old wardrobe.

Jessie would have loved a hot bath and a chance to wash her hair, but that would have to wait. She made do by stripping naked, filling the bowl with water from the pitcher, and sluicing down with a hand towel. Briskly she dried herself with the larger bath towel, her flesh tingling and glowing a healthy pink, then slipped on a floor-length peignoir. After brushing her hair and pinning it up, she doused the oil lamp and climbed between the covers. She fell into a deep slumber almost immediately.

Ki, too, had decided on a quick cat-bath. He peeled off his duds, washed, shaved and was working with the towel when he heard someone stop out in the hall.

"Ki?" Three taps sounded on the door. "Let me in."

Ki recognized Pru's whispered voice, but he didn't an-

Instinctively, his eyes checked to see that the
_ked and the window drapes were closed. If he
he'd keep it this way. In a small room the only
_er than a crossfire was a compromising situation.
y, Ki! Chita has eyes in back of her head, I

_-oh. Prudence had him skunked. Hurriedly Ki fished
_ean pants out of his valise and put them on for modesty.
Unlatching the door, he widened it just enough to let Pru
slip in, then immediately shut and bolted it.

"Well, at least now your housekeeper can't catch you
pounding on my door," Ki allowed, "and blame me for
luring you astray." He scratched his bare chest. "I wasn't
expecting visitors, especially ladies."

"Heavens, it isn't as though I haven't seen you in all
states of undress," Pru murmured, smoothing the folds of
her long, pink-striped nightgown. Her feet were bare, her
hair was freshly combed, and there seemed to be a coy
gleam to her eyes as she sidled close. "Fact is, it's you
who should be thinking improper of me, coming in alone
when everybody is asleep."

"No such notion ever dawned on me. But what is it you
want?"

"What do I want?" She licked her lips with the tip of
her tongue, a strange huskiness to her voice. "Lord, what
d'you suppose I want?"

"Revenge."

It was not exactly what she had in mind, he knew, but
it'd do her good to busy her wits over something. Something else, that is, besides a repetition of her prior visit
three years ago, and their meetings a time or two before
that. Yet despite his best intentions, Ki looked at Pru and
felt a stirring of those same old impulses. Perversely, it
wasn't his resolve he found was stiffening.

"Revenge, indeed," she pouted. "You're impossible."
Then in all seriousness she said, "Retribution, Ki. Yes, I

want to pay those killers back for butchering my dad and who knows how many others. You don't approve?''

"I understand."

"But you don't approve. I bet Jessie understands and agrees, too."

"You've a lot in common. She isn't a clinging vine that needs a trellis for support, and neither are you. You both expect to settle your own accounts, to repay in like coin, measure for measure."

"What horse-slobber," she drawled, smiling. "Flattery gets you anywhere with me, my Asian stallion." She was quivering; she stroked a finger shakily across his bare chest and stomach. "And I'm your ol' gray mare."

"Not old, and not gray, and you're sure what you used to be."

Prudence laughed throatily, her pink tongue gliding across her lips again. "What I used to have is what I want, Ki. You." Suddenly she was against him, and her arms were up and around him, breasts rubbing his chest, a wild tremble shaking her whole body. And just as quickly his arms, swift and sure, went around her. His resolve and intentions were far, far away when his lips found hers.

He eased his hand between them and across the front of her nightgown. She wriggled some but didn't object, didn't say a word as he began massaging one of her breasts. After a long moment she broke the kiss and sighed, "Take me, take me bare. . . ."

Ki untied the ribbon at the throat of her gown and unhooked the little clasps of the bodice. Shrugging her shoulders, Pru slipped the gown off and let it blossom around her feet, exposing smooth, unblemished skin, pointed breasts tipped by raspberry-sized nipples, and a plump pudendum, with lips accentuated by a thin line of velvety curls.

She watched his fingers kneading her right nipple until it was firm and distended. Her breathing was growing heavier, and Ki could feel a sensual trembling to her body as he moved to her left nipple, his other hand roaming down to the V of her crotch. She brought her thighs together on his hand and held it there, squeezing.

"We're forgetting something," she moaned.

He picked her up then, her slender body light in his arms, and laid her gently on the bunk bed. Aroused, he hastened to shuck his pants while she gazed at him, her eyes growing smoky and hungry. She twisted, allowing Ki room as he crawled on the bed, spreading her legs slightly to allow him to caress her sensitive valley. She moved her hips a little in concert with his rubbing hand, her hand sliding between his legs in search of his swollen erection. "Make it," she whispered, stroking the shaft, "make it as good as last time."

Rising, hovering over Pru, Ki felt her thighs widen to cradle him, her ankles locking around his calves as he pressed down on her loins, inserting himself firmly. Thus entwined, they began a simple yet urgent flexing of buttocks, a hardening and softening of the muscles of the lower abdomen, a gentle rocking of one body impaled by another. Ki lowered his head and their mouths fused together. Their tongues touched and flicked in play, Ki beginning now to plunge deeper and more swiftly. Breathing raggedly, Pru shuddered and moaned in response to the erotic sensations coursing through her flesh. She pistoned her tightly gripping loins around his shaft in rhythm to his quickening thrusts, until the bedsprings were squealing in protest.

Grinding against him, squirming with each sliding jolt, Prudence reached her climax, her fist stuffed in her mouth while she tried to stifle her cries of wanton ecstasy. Clenching his teeth, Ki felt his orgasm welling up, triggered by the clenching convulsions of her spasms. He flowed deep inside her, flooding her. Pru splayed her legs wide, arching up with pressuring force to milk his tide between her legs.

Slowly Ki settled down over her soft warm body, mash-

40

ing her breasts and belly with his weight, until his immediate satiation began to wane. Finally he withdrew and pressed alongside her, caressing her breasts.

"Mmm . . . They've been missing their bosom buddy, Ki."

"How about a kissing cousin?" he asked, his mouth closing on one of the nipples, sucking while he fondled her other breast.

"Not funny. Cousin Vaughn would like nothing better than to have friendly relations."

"Nothing doing?"

Pru shook her head. "I like Vaughn, I trust him and respect his advice, but he . . . Well, he's family."

"Do you trust all your crew like kin, too?"

"What do you mean?"

Ki shrugged. "A pack of bandidos tried a drygulch play in Persimmon Gap, but we fought them off. Before that Jessie noticed a *mestizo* loafer at Fort Pena, who rode away after she'd been asking about Ingot and Mashed-O. Seems like he must've been posted at Fort Pena to report travelers like us, or any strangers heading down into this country."

"But . . . but nobody knew you were coming!"

"Nobody knew precisely who or when." Ki's smile was mirthless. "And I'm sure when you wired Jessie to send someone quick, nobody knew outside Mashed-O. Yet your enemies were prepared for us, with lookout and trap all set. There's only one answer—a leak. Maybe it was just blabbed, or maybe it was tipped by somebody here on the take."

"I don't believe it!"

"Well, we'll find out in due time," Ki allayed, hugging her, advising, "Keep an open mind," as they lay that way, aware of each other and stirred by the closeness. "Keep your eyes and ears open, and keep your lips closed, too."

"And my legs?" she purred teasingly. "They won't

keep closed. But I'll keep them open as long as you keep it up."

She kept her promise. Pru was a wildly carnal young woman, with rampant imagination and energy. She rode him on top the second time. The third time she awakened Ki from a drowsy half-sleep with her hot lips. She was brazenly aggressive aboard him, now squatting astride his hips while leaning back, now lying full length, gasping, clinging, until another release left them both weak and exhausted.

Some time toward dawn, Prudence rolled from his bed, put on her nightgown, and silently departed. Ki didn't know when, but he sensed the loss. . . .

Come morning, Jessie arose early, but Ki and Pru got off to a slow start. After breakfast, they went to fetch their horses from the corral, Jessie taking no notice of Ki hobbling slightly, or of Pru mincing bowlegged—just as she'd taken no notice of the tempestuous romp that had resounded all night from the next room. Pru roped a taffy-maned sorrel, and they began saddling up.

Vaughn Yarbrough came over, leading a moro with tan leggins. Pru smiled him a greeting, but it was apparent he was deep in morning-after misery, sunk by more than the wine last night. Brusquely exchanging regards with Jessie and Ki, he talked of mundane ranch doings with Pru and helped them finish saddling. When they set out, Yarbrough rode along. He hadn't asked, and Pru hadn't said, yet he joined in as though it was his right and duty. Maybe it was. As cousins, Yarbrough could have a right of kin, and considering how Hugo Oliver was butchered, Yarbrough could feel a duty to guard Pru. Still, that was no way for a foreman to treat his boss, especially in company . . . but Jessie made no comment.

They headed south down Mooneye Valley, the morning sun still low on the eastern horizon, and as yet the killing heat of the day had not come. Presently they neared a sizable stream of swift water that ran along on their left.

There was good grass clothing the bank of the water, and plenty of groves yonder to make shade in the hot weather, and beyond were cool deep canyons to hole up in against the sun in summer and the snows in winter. To Jessie's practiced eye, this was richer than first appeared, and allowed all of creation for grazing beefs.

From the crest of a rise they saw, several miles to the southwest, most of Mashed-O's herd still bunched on a broad, tree-dotted pasture that flanked the stream.

"They've been herded together so long, they haven't taken to scattering much yet," Pru observed.

Ki eyed the cattle thoughtfully. "A close herd stampedes easily."

"Assumin' so," Yarbrough said, "so what? Ain't nothing here that'd make those scrubs turn tail, excepting . . ." He horselaughed. "You can't be thinking of rustlers, Ki. Who'd be interested in heisting such a sorry lot of ga'nted culls? After they get some meat on their bones, it'll be different, maybe."

"Lean cows travel well, and they can be fattened anywhere there's good grass and water," Ki argued.

"And there's plenty of both across the Rio," Jessie added.

Pru frowned quizzically. "What're you driving at, Jessie?"

"Well, if you'd sold to me and I owned that herd, I wouldn't leave it unguarded, particularly at night, long as it showed a tendency to bunch. I'd hide men here at night, too, and rig a trap with the cows as bait."

"Maybe it'd even a score or two. . . ." Pru conjectured, and after mulling it over, she turned to Yarbrough. "Vaughn, I think we should try what Jessie says. From tonight on, let's have some hands here covering the herd."

Yarbrough looked disgusted. "C'mon, Pru. Nobody with as much brains as a terrapin would bother lifting that pile of scrawny soupbones. F'get it."

Pru stared at Yarbrough. And something seemed to snap

43

inside her—like the spring of an old watch, Ki sensed; bang, thataway. "Maybe nobody will try. Maybe you're right, Vaughn, maybe it's a dumb folly by two giddy nincompoops," she said, her voice like the whetting of a sythe. "That's not the point. The point is, Vaughn, that I think you should try what I say."

"Point taken," Yarbrough said woodenly. "You want it, you got it."

"And who knows, there might be something in it," Pru remarked, softening her tone. "The hills off south aren't so far away, and a herd run into them by rustlers who know every crack and cranny would be mighty hard to catch."

As they rode on, Jessie gazed southward toward the grim battlements of the Espantosa Hills. Domed and spired, slashed with gorges and canyons, the jagged ruddy-colored bedrock was thickly grown with chaparral. In the harsh glare of the mounting sun they had a sinister, barbaric cast, as if their gaunt crags hid an ancient mystery.

After a distance the stream which flowed swiftly yet placidly down Mooneye Valley disappeared into one of the dour canyons. Scanning the dark mouth of the canyon as they passed, Jessie could envisage the stream changing to a fierce torrent that clove the stone hills to the Rio Grande. She broke the silence that had endured since they left the crest of the rise.

"How far do your holdings run?"

"According to the rancher Dad bought out, for about ten miles into the hills," Pru answered. "When Zed Rykoff first took title to this section, he included all the northern stretch of the hills. They're worthless for grazing, but he had an old chart showing there might be silver or other metal in them, like there is in the slopes to the northwest."

"Rykoff sure got the wrong slant," Yarbrough remarked. "They don't contain nothin' except bandit burrows, I reckon."

"He gave Dad the map, claiming it led nowhere but

44

went with the place,'' Pru added with a laugh. ''He said the Yaqui Indians used to have another name for the hills, too. They called them the 'Abode of the Mirror that Smokes.' ''

''Abode of the Mirror that Smokes?''

''Right, Jessie, that's what Rykoff said. What that could mean he didn't know, but it seems the Yaquis believed there was something sacred about them.'' Pru squinted up at the sun, which was nearing the noon apex. ''It's growing hot enough to boil the tallow out of my hide. Come on, let's head for home.''

As they swung their horses around, Jessie shifted in her saddle and again gazed at the seared barrier to the south, her brows furrowing slightly, her eyes narrowing thoughtfully, suspiciously . . .

There was nothing suspicious, however, that Jessie or Ki found about the Mashed-O crew. Although getting on in years, the hands were tough veterans and thoroughly competent to perform rangeland chores. But the grueling drive from the Nueces country had worn them down, and the double-whammy loss of their old foreman, Rye Flynn, and the head honcho himself, Hugo Oliver, had left them with little initiative. Still, they gave every appearance of being loyal to the brand and devoted to Miss Pru, and reasonably contented to take orders from Flynn's successor, Cousin Vaughn.

''Yarbrough's run his own spread and savvies punchin','' one of the crew told Ki. ''He don't always boss things same's Flynn—can't be expected to—but he don't cater to suggestions, or stand for no foolishness.''

One chore that Yarbrough insisted upon caused some grumbling at first. Following through on his promise to Prudence, each night he assigned hands to guard the still-bunched cattle on the southwest pasture. He did not have his nighthawks ride herd in the usual manner, but ordered them to hole up in the thickets, out of sight, from just after nightfall to the first streak of dawn. Naturally the crew didn't cotton to the task over much, and were as dubious as Yarbrough of the reasons behind it. But when they discovered that Miss Pru was steadfastly supporting it, and that Ki was backing the idea by working on the job with them, they made the best of it.

One moonless black night, the apparently needless caution was justified. The Mashed-O hawks were hunched in their saddles in the shelter of a thicket, slapping at gnats and mosquitoes, and yearning for the consolation of the cigarettes they did not dare light. Ki sat his horse a little in advance of the hands, watching the shadowy mass of bunched cattle, not so large a herd as formerly, for by now many of the cows had begun drifting off over the range.

All of a sudden, without warning, a wild pandemonium broke loose in the vicinity of the herd. From a nearby grove flitted moving shadows. The air quivered to the roar of gunfire, the rataplan of hooves, the howling yells.

The cattle came to their feet with bellows of alarm. They plunged wildly in bewildered confusion. Out of the concealing thicket tore Mashed-O waddies, guns blazing. The exultant whoops of the rustlers turned to startled yells and screams of pain. Confused, panic-stricken, tangled up with the stampeding cattle, they fought madly to flee as the Mashed-O bullets whistled about their ears.

Ki led the counter-attack, well in front of the crew. He had almost reached the fringes of the herd when a horseman loomed gigantic in the dust-clouded darkness. It was too late to pull aside. With a crash that knocked both animals off their feet, the two charging mounts met shoulder to shoulder.

Ki had barely time to kick his feet free from the stirrups and hurl himself sideward. He hit the ground with stunning force. At the same instant the other rider thudded beside him within arm's length. Ki slashed a vicious blow at the man's dimly seen head, dropping him flat. But the rustler reached up and seized Ki's descending wrist in a grip of steel. Ki felt his wrist bones grind together, and in sharp

46

agony, he whipped his left hand over and chopped at the other man's chest, buckling him gasping and tearing loose his hold.

The force of the blow and some treacherous gravel underfoot caught Ki off balance, sending him sprawling from his awkward position on one knee. His head banged against a rock and a flash of blackness rolled over him. It was gone in a moment, but before his brain cleared the rustler had scrambled to his feet and vanished into the darkness. An instant later Ki heard the thud of swift hooves a little to the right.

By the time Ki retrieved his hammerhead roan, which fortunately had not been injured by the fall, the thudding hoofbeats were dying swiftly into the night. "Damn, what a grip that bastard has," Ki muttered, wincing as he swung asaddle, his fingers still numb and his wrist feeling as if it were broken.

From down the valley he could hear the Mashed-O nighthawks shouting and cursing. Some of them were fighting to turn the stampeding herd, while others were chasing with guns ablaze after the fleeing rustlers. Ki joined the pursuit.

In short time they had come close to the first stony heights of the Espantosa Hills, and still the dust-pluming trail was fresh and unmistakable. They plunged into an arroyo, Ki repressing an impulse to warn of ambush, although the broken rock and ledges made the area perfect for such a move. Soon they reached an open plain, and Ki glimpsed hard-riding figures yonder ahead. A puff of smoke arose and a distant howl of defiance echoed in the air.

"We've caught up with 'em!" an exultant cowhand shouted.

The rustlers veered away, swinging eastward. The Mashed-O band poured after them, yelling recklessly above the pounding of the hooves. Abruptly the rustlers whirled and leveled rifles. They fired at long range, but the bullets came close enough to slow up and scatter the Mashed-O pursuers. Instantly the rustlers set spurs and continued their flight.

After that Ki could only catch glimpses of the rustlers in the twisting, rock-strewn canyons. The Mashed-O pressed eagerly ahead, in a circuitous course that as best he could determine was bringing them back around to the south and west again. The rustlers disappeared around yet another turn and when they were seen again, they were streaking down a long, narrow straight stretch. Now it was the Mashed-O's turn to loosen a salvo of rifle shots. A number of the fast moving outlaws jerked, crying out, their horses swerving and breaking stride for a moment. Some fell from their perches, while others hung on, picking up the pace, spurring deeper and disappearing around another bend.

The Mashed-O pursuers rounded it soon afterward and abruptly drew rein. Ahead was a wide slope down to the Rio Grande. Across the river the adobes of a Mexican village huddled. The rustlers struck the water with a sheet of spray and plunged across into Mexico. Blistering the air with curses and gunpowder, the Mashed-O fired shot after shot until the escaping wideloopers had been swallowed by darkness and distance.

Returning to Mooneye Valley, they joined the other nighthawks in rounding up the cattle. Already most of the outside stragglers had been cut in, and the leaders had been turned until a column was forming like a capital letter *U*. Soon the two ends were merged together, and the more compact mass was racing in a circle. It did not take much of this milling to exhaust the cows. Finally they shambled to a snorting, blowing halt, and the stampede was over.

It was almost dawn when Ki and the Mashed-O rode into the ranch quarters. Their news rousted everyone and led to a sleepy-eyed but alert gathering in the parlor of the ranchhouse.

"Ki, you sure figured it right, but how you figured it is

beyond me," Yarbrough said. "This just naturally don't make sense."

Jessie agreed with the foreman; it didn't make sense. Nobody who wasn't loco would take a chance on stealing cows in the shape the Mashed-O's were, as she and Ki were both well aware. Contrary to their earlier arguments, which they'd couched to avoid spilling all their notions, they very well knew that rustlers didn't wideloop cattle to fatten them up, but grabbed fat beefs which could be turned over quick for top price. The whole thing tonight showed poor judgment—from that point of view.

"What was that town across the Rio?" Ki asked. "And what do you know of it?"

"Quevidas?" Pru said. "Like the other ranchers around, we've a lot of suspicions, but that's all. It's been a hangout for border thieves, but I gather there's never been a trace of wet cattle found over there. Most folks are most suspicious of the Brazos Kid."

Jesse frowned. "What's his real name?"

"I've never heard any other. He owns the Gridiron, a hardscrabble spread verging on the Rio Grande, not far from where those rustlers crossed over. I gather he's refused to help any other ranchers and spends much of his time in Quevidas."

"If his brand resembles a gridiron, your Brazos Kid would be able to blotch over most brands, like a rustler's running iron," Ki noted, rubbing an earlobe. "Offhand, the gent and that town, Quevidas, are too close to things not to be involved somehow. Looks like they'd be worth watching, Jessie."

"They do," she agreed, adding with grim satisfaction, "In fact, there're several angles that need to be covered. The rustlers tipped their hand. They were aiming to cripple the Mashed-O so Prudence would go bust and have to quit. Somebody doesn't want her in Mooneye Valley. But in the name of blazes, why?"

★

Chapter 4

Ki rode back to the Rio Grande. There was much to do with little time to do it, and besides, by the look in Prudence's eyes, he wouldn't have gotten any sleep if he'd gone to bed. Splashing across the river where the bandidos had fled into Mexico, he tracked unmapped mesa and arroyo toward a glint of lights that marked the outlaw roost of Quevidas. The lights seemed closer than they were, and dawn was commencing to gray out the stars when he threaded between dingy shuttered buildings and *jacal*-style mud hovels along the only street.

No law existed down here beyond the law of survival, the right of might, so Ki entered boldly as any gringo renegade with a price on his head. He reined up in the central plaza, glancing nonchalantly around while watering his horse at a masonry ditch that fed a large, squarish trough. The plaza fronted an ancient building of adobe and mountain pine, built in the form of a square with a patio in the middle. It appeared to originally have been a *residencia* of some long dead *patrón* or cattle *barón*, but now half the building had been turned into a granary, storehouse, and stable, with the big salon in use as a cantina. There were no hombres drunk or sober in sight, only some bedraggled washerwomen scrubbing clothes in the trough, breasts sagging beneath loose *camisas*, a few scruffy mules standing about for no apparent reason, and a scavenging hound dog.

And suddenly the ragged young boy. He came hustling out from a corner of the building, barefoot with a single rope suspender to hold his pants up. "Help with your horse, señor?" he begged, doffing his straw hat and holding it in his hands. "For five centavos I will unsaddle your horse, señor."

Dismounting, Ki flipped him an American five-cent piece. "Show me where."

"*En sequida*—at once!"

Taking the horse by its reins, the lad crossed the hardpan that served as a sidewalk, leading Ki around behind the cantina to some pole and adobe horse sheds. Nobody seemed to be at the cantina, though a light was burning inside. But from the other end of the sprawling old building, a bedroom wing with iron grillework over the open windows, came occasional laughs and feminine shrieks, and the liquid strum of a guitar being played rapidly in fandango rhythm. Upward of a dozen mustangs were tied along racks nearby, so evidently their owners, *vaqueros* or *bandidos*, were making a night of it with the local talent.

The lad misread Ki's glance at the windows. "Don't pay them a visit," he said, curling his lip. "They're all *brujas enfermas*—diseased hags. If you desire a girl, my sister is bella, a virgin, almost."

"I'm sure she is." Grinning, Ki had the boy hitch his horse away from the others, then removed the saddle and bridle. After a quick rubdown, he replaced the gear using an "owlhoot" rig with loose cinches and bit free, but hanging so it could be instantly slipped into place.

52

"You'll find her in the cantina, señor. Waiting, at a side table."

"Who's she waiting for?"

"Perhaps for you."

Ki chuckled softly and spun him another coin. "Why, yes. Maybe she is. Quien sabe?"

With a flash of even teeth startling white in his sunbrowned face, the urchin darted off. Ki walked over to the cantina, ducking beneath a pole awning and glancing inside. The room was wide and low, its ceiling supported by dozens of fancy carved pillars, gilded once, but now tarnished from generations of tobacco smoke. At one end was a plain counter with a piece of rusty mirror behind it. Overhead hung four candles in a suspension holder, illuminating the counter well enough, falling on the head and shoulders of a dozing bartender. But the light played out rapidly across the room and left the far walls shrouded in gloom.

It appeared empty, except for the bartender. Ki went around to the patio where a second door led inside. He saw her then, seated at a table by the far wall, looking tired and bored.

He paused, pleasantly surprised. Disregarding how almost a virgin she may have been, the lad had been truthful about his sister—she cut a helluva fine figure of a young woman. Black tangled hair, shot with sunbleached tendrils, framed a vivid face with a full mouth that was almost too wide, and brooding eyes that were dark and moist, like olives. She wore slim leather huaraches, and an embroidered plum frock that seemed to accentuate more than conceal her long legs, ripe thighs and lush, succulent breasts.

No one save the girl and the bartender. Ki moved inside, keeping more or less to the shadows rearward of the pillars, and sat down against the wall.

Jerking awake when Ki entered, the bartender came from behind the counter, grumbling between his teeth. He was short, thin, and at first glimpse Ki took him to be another boy. Reflected candlelight then showed him to be a stringy, rodent-faced man of peon stock with tiny brass rings in his ears. Thrust in a sash at his waist was an old, double-barreled percussion cap pistol, heavy and slow to get into action, but capable of turning a man's belly inside-out.

"Tequila," Ki ordered, surveying the cantina in disdain. "Hell, no gals, no music, only four candles for light . . . Ain't a goddamn thing here."

The bartender shrugged. "Quevidas ver' small, ver' poor."

"Too bad. Possibly you could use some extra *pesos*, eh?" Ki gave him a foxy grin, saying no more till the bartender fetched a bottle and glass. Then handing him a gold dollar, he divulged, "I want to buy cattle, some good stock that would've— eh—wandered across the river and been picked up as strays."

The bartender looked blank. *"Señor, no entiendo."*

"Well, if you don't understand, let me talk to the owner."

"I am the owner, Felipe Murillo. And you?"

"Smith. John Smith."

"Here all gringos are named John Smith."

"Here everything is for sale."

"So gringos believe, but this time you are wrong."

"Listen, I ain't on the prod against those who—strayed with the cattle. That ain't my business. The price of beef is, if it's cheap enough."

"No cows here," Murillo replied, looking sorrowful. "Drink is here in my cantina, señor, that's all I know. Maybe next town, no?"

Ki made an impatient gesture. "Okay, play safe. I'll hang around a few days and fine someone in this section who'll sell me a bunch of lost dogies."

"Por dios, you have the welcome." Shrugging again, elaborately, Murillo returned to the bar.

Ki toyed with his glass, drinking very little, aware of Murillo's dark, suspicious eyes watching his every move. The girl ignored him, figuring he'd be harder to sucker than she cared to try. She was waiting, all right—for quitting time. Ki had known too many like her, typical daughters of frontier entertainment, not to savvy her drift. On the whole, he liked her type. They didn't fool with that innocent prude routine of coyness and teasing. When they had an interest in you, they showed it, and when they didn't, that ended it.

Bearing them both in mind, Ki edged over a few tables to a better vantage point. He settled in for a stay, hoping for a break. He discounted Murillo's denials about the cattle and reckoned his chances for catching a lead were as good here as anywhere, at least for the moment.

At the moment he could hear the guitar being played in faster rhythm, a tarantella with men's drunken harmony garbling it. There were also sounds of some woman dancing violently on a table, and other, wilder noises echoing from the far wing of the building, an increasing racket that grew until the whole hurraw climaxed in a knife brawl. Then it hushed right down again.

The moment stretched on . . . while dawn grew up across the barren hills, lighting the flat adobe structures, but making the cantina's interior seem darker than ever. . . .

Then loud and abrupt, some of the rowdies at the other end spilled outside into the plaza. Boots thumping, big-roweled spurs jangling, they could be heard coming along the front of the building toward the cantina, palavering coarsely in border Spanish with drawling laughter and incessant profanity.

One of the voices dominated the others, and the girl seemed to recognize it. She turned a trifle in her chair, stiffening a little, watching the door when they clomped in. Three of them. Bearded, unkempt, heavily armed, with that feral-eyed stamp of border renegades.

Ki instantly recognized the swaggering leader of the trio

as the bandido who had bossed the ambush at Persimmon Gap. At close range he looked uglier than ever. His face was flat and massive, bristle-bearded, a jagged knife scar puckering the skin near his left eye. His hamhock hands glittered with gold and silver rings, and there were gold rings in his ears, too. His trousers, dirty and drooping, had been costly once, cream and brown with gold braid down each leg. Around his waist hung two belts heavy with cartridges and holstered Dragoons. He also carried a sheath knife on each belt, another partly concealed at the back of his neck, and most likely one in each boot, Ki reckoned. The total weight of guns, knives, and cartridges must have topped twenty pounds, but he swaggered under the load with the carelessness of long habit.

Noticing neither Ki nor the girl, he stalked across the room to the bar. "Pulque! Pronto!" He beat on the counter with forearm and fist, striking it so hard that dust rose from the floor. "You hear, Felipe, *mi amigo*? Pulque to wash the *sirup de amor* from my mouth. Pulque for these brave *soldados* who mounted many assaults last night, and a toast for those who're still charging with lances high!"

Right, Ki thought; there must be eight or nine more renegades left at the other end, estimating by the horses out back. He began to wonder if coming here was such a smart idea.

The bandido tossed down a tumbler of pulque, wiped thick lips on the back of his hand, and turned, hitching the weight of guns and cartridge belts. It was then he spotted the girl. "Evita!" Flashing her a cheezy grin, he tossed his anthill sombrero on the counter and strutted toward her, hands on his hips. "What would an evening be without my Evita?"

Evita did not respond. The girl was still sitting, apparently in the same posture, one hand on the table, the other in her lap. Her lips were drawn thin, the corners of her mouth twisted down showing her contempt for him, for them all.

56

Ki slid back in his chair, a movement that freed his vest. He had no immediate intention of intervening or disclosing his presence, but it merely made him feel better to be ready. He simply sat, tilted a trifle back in the chair, watching the bandido chief and the girl.

"I have a few coins left. I always do, for you," the bandido said, jingling the change in his pants pocket. "Always enough to sit with *mi favorita* and share us a drink."

"You are not my favorite, Luiz Zugate." Her voice was brittle as crystal. "I am tired of hearing you. I am tired of looking at your foolish face. I am tired of smelling your clothes filled with horse's sweat. If you wish to sit and drink together with me, it will cost you. A—a thousand pesos."

"Ho! And who are you to demand a perfumed Don?" Zugate paused across the table from her. "Behold your poor Luiz, who's ridden long and hard in the saddle las' night. Is it not so, *compañeros*?" he roared to his men.

His men shouted agreement, laughing and beating fists on the bar.

Turning to glance back at them, Zugate caught sight of Ki. He hesitated, casting Ki a quick searching look with his black squinty eyes. "I seen you one night before, *japonés*, over the edge of my gunsights."

"And last night, riding long and hard away from those of the Mashed-O's," Ki responded evenly. "Why? What's your game?"

For an instant Zugate seemed puzzled, but then he chortled in his heavy throat. "My game is my business, yes? I do it again maybe."

"When?"

The laugh grew, mirthless, malicious. "Do not bother me now." Zugate hooked a chair with his boot toe, spun it around, and sat down, his weight creaking the chair. "Wine, Felipe. Your best wine for me and *mi chiquita*."

Murillo hastened over, trying to draw a cork from a

bottle of cheap plonk. Cursing, Zugate seized the bottle, set it on the table, and shattered the neck with a blow from one of his Dragoons. He then poured two glasses full to the brim and lifted one in his thick fingers.

"To Evita. To *la gatita*—the pussy—who is match for Luiz Zugate."

He had paid her the supreme compliment at his disposal, and now he waited, beaming, for her response. She lifted the glass, not to her lips, but level with her right ear. Zugate suddenly realized that she was going to throw it, but he did not move. He sat as he had been, an expression of set truculence on his lips, and took the wine across the face.

"Ha!" he hissed the syllable. "You jaguar! You would spit in the face of Il Diablo, no?"

"Pay me the thousand pesos!"

Zugate planted massive forearms on the table, eyes on her face. "Perhaps, for *you*, one thousand pesos. I might do this even after this, because I like spirit. In horse, even in man I shoot, do I like spirit." He leaned across, wine gathering in big drops on his beard and falling from his chin, running down his thick neck, staining his shirt and fancy-braided pants. "But mostly of all do I like spirit in *las demas bonitas*—beautiful women."

Her lips tried to form a word that would show her contempt. *"Marica. Marica barato."*

Zugate gawked, face sagging. Apparently he had not expected a second rebuff, much less to be called—to put it most kindly— an effeminate tightwad. He licked his lips, glanced around at Ki and his men at the bar. They had heard, and their hearing had wounded his prestige. He lunged to his feet.

The girl saw Zugate coming and was up ahead of him, but not quite fast enough. He grabbed her by the arm, dragged her forward. For a moment she was against him, then with feline quickness she twisted away. Her hand came up, raking his cheek. They left streaks that were white for an instant, then red as they filled with blood.

He still held her with one hand, rubbed the other across his beard, drew it away and stared at the slick smear of blood. She stood still, panting through clenched teeth, then with a sharp movement bent down and away, and her arm slipped from his fingers.

He started after her. A chair was in his way. He trod it underfoot, smashing it to splintered rungs. "Ho! Señorita of the long claws. Sometime already have I tamed wildcats to lap milk and walk on string at my heels."

Evita moved back, making an effort to elude him along the wall. But Zugate, pouncing, was all over her, seizing her wrists and forcing them behind her. She writhed back and forth, teeth bared, to no avail. Brutally he forced her arms together, got hold of both wrists in one hand, leaving his other free.

The girl's futile struggles did something to Zugate. His eyes brightened, became triumphant and gloating in the midst of his broad, blood-smeared face. He was breathing hard through his nostrils. "Behold now your Luiz, your Don who no one dare say smell like sweat of horse. Who must have woman worthy of him to sit at his table."

Her frock was ripped. His hand came up, ripping it farther, revealing the swell of her plump, golden breasts almost to the nipples.

"See? You will be this woman. Like woman in ballroom gown, with hair on shoulder. So thus you shall sit at my table." He bent over, pressed his lips against the flesh of her right breast. She fought him, but his lips were still pressed leaving a smear of his blood. . . .

Ki was on his feet, crossing the room. The two bandidos at the bar saw him and shouted a warning, drawing weapons as they rushed to block his way. Zugate became aware of him. He jerked his head up, backed away, dragging the girl by her two wrists, his free hand swinging down for a Dragoon.

59

The closer of the two bandidos charged with his arm raised, gripping a bowie-style butcher knife. The other, angling to blast Ki in a crossfire, was thumbing the gunhammer of a vintage Remington .44. With a sharp twisting of his body to the left, Ki threw a right-forearm block to deflect the slashing knife blade, and countered by ramming the heel of his left palm in a *teisho* blow to the man's nose. He saw the brutal features contort with startled pain, and heard the satisfying sound of cartilage splitting. The man's head flew back, shards of fractured nasal bone spearing up into his brain. His honed steel blade sliced past the corded muscles of Ki's belly, arching harmlessly to the floor.

Dead on his feet, the man began crumpling. Ki was already pivoting to the other man, following through with a catlike shift to lash out with a snap-kick to the solar plexus. Clutching his hemmorhaging belly, the second bandido fell to his knees, his pistol dropping from nerveless fingers.

Luiz Zugate, a Dragoon clutched in his hamhock fist, swiveled for a point-blank shot at Ki. It exploded, whipping lead and burning powder, but the girl had ruined his aim, her head darting down, sharp teeth sinking into his gunwrist. Pain and surprise made him release her.

And Ki, launching into a *tobi-geri* flying kick, sailed across the short remaining distance and slammed Zugate in the chest with his extended left foot. His ferocious spring buckled Zugate, carrying him reeling backward toward the bar, his Dragoon firing again with a deafening roar alongside Ki's ear.

Felipe Murillo dived headlong out of the way, barely in time. Zugate smashed hard against the counter, splintering planks and shattering bottles, landing flat in a horrendous geyser of wood, glass, booze and dust. Groggy but not unconscious. He had a brute brain, impervious to punishment.

The girl saw his Dragoon on the floor. Ki seized her arm and tried to force her toward the door, but she twisted away from him with a mountain-cat strength that took him by surprise.

"Get out of here!" he yelled.

"Leave me alone. I do not need your help. I need no man's help!"

Murillo was beside the ruins of his bar, enraged but lacking the guts to go for his pistol. The bandido with the knife still lay where he'd died, but the other bandido was nowhere in sight.

Ki took a step to one side—glimpsed him. A shine of gunmetal. He knew the bandido's old Remington was aimed at him. Explosion. It was Zugate's Dragoon, which the girl fired without turning, aiming across her waist beneath an uplifted left arm.

The heavy slug struck, spinning the bandido halfway around. The Remington dangled in his fingers as he stood with his shoulders propped against a pillar. Then, with a foolish, slack-jawed expression, he slid to a sitting position with legs thrust straight out, his peso-toweled spurs digging little grooves across the floor.

The blast of gunfire seemed to bring Zugate around. He started fumbling to his hands and knees, then stopped, looking up into the round muzzle of his own revolver. His heavy, bloody face contorted into a sort of crazed grimace. "Ho! Ho! What woman. What woman for Don Luiz."

Evita let him crawl toward her a few feet. Her finger squeezed the trigger, sending a bullet that tore splinters from the floor between Zugate's hands. He kept on coming.

"What woman for Don—"

She backed away, the gun rocking again, again, smashing dust and splinters into his bloody face. At the door she hesitated to scan the room, then backed to the patio.

Ki was there ahead of her, covering her retreat without drawing attention to his presence. He walked with long strides to the patio's rear exit and waited there. His voice came from the shadows, "You better pull that trigger one more time, Evita. Once through the *cabeza*. That's where you shoot rattlesnakes, through the *cabeza*."

She had not seen him in the deep shadow. Startled, she leaped aside, swinging the heavy Dragoon, its barrel aimed directly between his eyes. "A fine man to talk. Bouncing around at him unarmed!" Laughing then, she lowered the gun, and tucked a stray wisp of hair back with her other hand. "Would you have me shoot all the snakes in Quevidas, Señor Gringo? And if I did, how many more would breathe here with the dawn tomorrow?"

He watched her back away through the patio door, then turn and hurry to the adobe stable. A moment later she galloped out on a head-slinging mustang, her body sleek and supple, integrated with every movement of the stolen horse as she disappeared around the side of the building.

Ki made no attempt to follow. Instead he rode north, skirting the plaza and hovels, and started back along the trail to the Rio Grande. Behind he heard the crack of a rifle and a bullet sang by his head. Instantly he yanked his Winchester Express from the saddle scabbard and twisted around, glimpsing Luiz Zugate at the doorway of the distant cantina. The Winchester went up to Ki's shoulder and spat flame. Plaster adobe jumped beside the Mexican bandido's head and he dodged for the safety of the door.

Ejecting the shell, Ki sat still, looking back for a moment. Zugate didn't appear again. With a faint smile, Ki heeled his mount and continued on. Shortly, approaching the river, he noticed a place where the north bank rose sharply so that a man and his horse could easily be concealed. From there he could watch the sure to come pursuit. In case he was already being watched, he gave no sign of his discovery as he waded into the river.

Crossing in safety, Ki urged his horse straight ahead. In a few moments he was swallowed by a dark canyon, and pushing on, he found a little side path that led to the sheltered pocket behind the high bank he had spotted. Dismounting, he made his horse comfortable and climbed the bank to where he could watch the ford across the Rio. He settled in, patiently waiting.

He did not have to wait long. With a ground-swelling rumble, he heard the thunder of horse hooves, the wrench of saddles, the guttural profanities of approaching riders. Focusing on the far sweep of the trail, he saw Zugate and his remaining renegades careen around the bend, brandishing rifles and setting up a howl as they splashed across the river. On the American side, they reined up in a gesticulating group around Zugate, who dispatched them in twos and threes in various directions.

Ki stayed put, watching. So did Zugate, staring after his men until they were gone from sight, and then spurring on up into the canyon. Alone. The dun stallion he rode was slightly larger and heavier than most, but his size made it seem burro-small. The huge pointed sombrero on his head, the trapaderos that almost brushed the grass, the serape over his shoulder and all the load of guns and belts made the horse seem even smaller.

Zugate approached within a hundred yards of Ki, then angled off, and in a quarter of an hour dropped over a bulge of the country. Ki slid down the bank, drew the latigo of his saddle tight, remounted, and took his time about following. He reached the bulge of country, but Zugate was already lost from view.

Tracks led around the face of a mesa, and west toward nearby Boquillas Canyon, that devil's country of border strip where five men could laugh at a regiment. Following, Ki made every unpredictable turn as the tracks took him on a zigzag course up and down and through the mountainous barrens of sand and wind-blasted rock.

As morning grew into afternoon, he descended into an arroyo that became progressively deeper, the bottom almost impenetrable from thorn. Presently he drew up at sight of a corral and a shack of a house, akin more to a line-cabin or miner's shanty than a ranch dwelling. He dismounted, went afoot, and finally he lay belly down across the hot dirt and stones of the arroyo side and peered down through parted cactus swords.

He'd been closer to Luiz Zugate than he thought. The bandido chief had dismounted and was turning his stallion loose in the tiny corral. There was a second horse in the enclosure, saddled. Someone was evidently waiting for him.

Zugate dropped the corral bar once more in place and stalked heavy and bowlegged toward the shack. A canteen was hanging on a peg. He drank from it, hung it back, called that he was coming in. His voice was a snarl. It was a voice to go with his face, which by now had swollen to something scarcely resembling a man's. An answer came from a man within the shack, and Zugate stomped inside, slamming the door behind him.

Ki eased back out of sight, climbed the arroyo side until the bulge of it let him stand upright. Then he circled and moved down directly toward the shack, sitting, digging his heels into the steep slope, taking care not to dislodge a pebble or stream of dirt that would betray him.

The shack roof came in view, but he kept going, clinging to the sheer slope, and at last found foot support and a measure of concealment behind some thorny mesquite. Through the thin wall he could hear the two men inside, their talk muffled yet discernible.

". . . he will come. You can't let him nose around, Luiz. Too much depends upon it."

"Señor, this gringo, he's already been there."

"Damn you, why didn't you get him?" the other man snapped in Spanish. Ki couldn't identify the speaker, other than by the inflection in his voice that he was American. "This makes twice you've failed, you bungler."

Zugate spat in disgust. "He not fight fair, señor. He use the body, *por dios*, like a cannonball."

"Of all the loco plays."

"It is not so bad. My men, they look for him now. They catch him and then he's not bother us no more."

64

"Maybe," the other man answered skeptically. "Now you listen to me, Luiz. Prudence Oliver's brought him and that Starbuck dame down here, snooping into who killed her ol' man. We're going to hit the Mashed-O again and here's what we'll do. You go to—"

At this moment Ki's keen ears heard a slight movement behind him. He whirled, hand streaking for the weapons in his vest. As he half-expected, he saw a crouching figure and whipped a dagger at him. A howl of pain answered his fling. Ki left the wall in a crouching run, heading toward the arroyo bank and his horse. He heard Zugate's bellow as the bandido chief burst out of the cabin. A gun blasted, then another—no doubt from the other, unknown man—as lead was triggered in a haphazard if concerted salvo. Bullets nipped at his heels, spanged off rocks next to him, clipped his clothing—

Then one slug cut a glancing swath along his right temple. He never heard it, but felt it like the blow of a mallet, and saw it as lights flashed blindingly in his skull. It sent him falling, spinning down . . . down . . . into abysmal darkness, and he never knew when he hit the ground. . . .

★

Chapter 5

"Somebody doesn't want the Mashed-O on this range here. But in the name of blazes, why . . . ?"

In search of the answer to her question, Jessie headed for Ingot, leaving the ranch about the same time Ki arrived in Quevidas. Upon reaching the mining town, she had a bedside visit with Gotch-ear Gillespie, who was recuperating nicely. Gotch-ear had the bartender Sam go fetch Zed Rykoff for her, but otherwise he wasn't able to be of much help. His notion that outlaws down in the Espantosa Hills just naturally didn't want close neighbors wouldn't hold water. For, as Jessie pointed out:

"Rustlers wouldn't want to run livestock raising off a range. Fat beefs are their business, and unless there are ranches to grow them, good cattle don't thrive."

Introduced by Sam, Zed Rykoff proved to be an elderly cowman, gristled and grizzled, with gray Dundrearie whiskers furring his caved-in cheeks. By that time, Jessie had obeyed Gotch-ear's nurse and left him to rest, and was once again seated in the parlor room of the Paydirt Bar. While waiting for Rykoff, she had watched the passing scene, keeping an eye peeled for Wade Duval. The Fortuna office manager had intrigued her, sparking a personal attraction that hinted of sexual arousal—not that she had any such designs in mind; it was one thing to admire the man and quite another to desire him. But there was no sign of Duval, though his boss, Big Nick Tualatin, and mine superintendent Leo Frost were in the Paydirt, playing poker at a nearby table. Tualatin muttered and glowered continually. Frost spoke rarely behind his perpetual smile, only his continual rolling, lighting, and smoking one cigarette after another betraying his nervous tension.

When Sam showed up with Rykoff, Jessie happened to be glancing out the parlor window, idly watching an ore-laden wagon rumble ponderously by to the stamp mill.

"The ore ain't rich in silver, but enough to turn a profit," Rykoff remarked, sitting down at her table. "Tualatin's Fortuna, which ain't an overly large holdin', does purty well, and so do a few other smallish digs. Everybody's always looking to hit a vein of high-grade, of course, and cash in big. Naturally, cow owners are doin' fine as things are, what with not having to ship much to outside markets an' all. Yep, Hugo Oliver moved here at a real smart time, Miz Starbuck. It's about him you're interested, ain't it?"

Jessie nodded. "I've come to beg a little information."

"Impartin' information is one of my favorite enjoyments." Fishing a pipe from his pocket, Rykoff explained the deal and liberal terms he'd arranged with Oliver, and was perfectly candid about his reasons for selling out.

"I would've hung on if it wasn't for the Espantosa Hills. I'd no need of the range when I bought it, but figured on using it later on. Now it's later on, and at my age, I don't hanker to get to feuding with owlhoots. They don't bother us so much up thisaway, 'cept for a raid now and then on our stock, but down in Mooneye Valley, everythin' is in their favor." Rykoff frowned, wadding tobacco in his pipe. "Two buyers before Oliver tried to squat there, but they didn't have no better luck. The first one built a good ranchhouse and barns and other buildin's. He lasted about as long as a rabbit in a hounddawg's mouth. The next feller is still down there, but he's planted beside a cottonwood, and ain't worryin' a sweat about what's goin' on around him."

"Knowing this, Oliver was still determined to make a go of it?"

"Mule stubborn, ma'am. Seein' as he was the third feller wanting to take over my land, I thought maybe he'd hold the lucky number and tough 'em out." Firing his pipe, Rykoff blew a sulfurous cloud of smoke. "If them rustlers leave his daughter alone, all she needs to do is fatten up her stock, and she's all set to start making money."

"I'm afraid Miss Oliver's almost lost her herd already," Jessie said, and briefly recounted the previous night's raid. "Evidently she's also lost the map you gave her father. Or maybe it was taken off him when he was killed. In any case, we can't find it."

"Sorry to hear of Miz Pru's troubles, but"—Rykoff chuckled—"that map ain't no loss. It's just one of those phony ol' prospecting charts that I got as a laugh from a drunk desert rat for the price of a whiskey. Believe me, it don't lead nowhere and don't make no sense, no matter which side you hold up."

"What did it look like? Can you recall?"

"Sure. I fooled over the map so much, combing the Espantosas, that every mark is nie branded on my bu—er, brain." Rykoff dug out a pencil stub and drew on the back of a scrap feed bill, then handed her the paper. "This's it."

Jessie stared curiously at his sketch, which seemed to be

a crude geologic map with formula. "Well," she said after a moment, "part of it makes sense."

"You savvy them hen scratches?" Rykoff was skeptical.

"Some. I learned to read maps on trips with my father to new projects and such," Jessie explained, and turned to his drawing. "These circular lines are evidently contours. They form two buttes or mesas here, the left one steeper, a trifle higher. And this deep arroyo, ripping smack down between them."

"An area like that could be anyplace in the hills."

"And the map doesn't show where." Jessie paused thoughtfully. "The only place I can think of is where the valley stream cuts through to the Rio. Could this deep arroyo be that big long gorge of the streambed?"

Rykoff shook his head. "Im-possible. A few miles in, the gorge walls drop plumb to the water, and it's just as sheer where the creek leaves at the south end of the hills. That means some two dozen miles of fast-surging current with no banks, caves, or ways up between the water and the cliffs."

Nodding, Jessie studied the map. "Now, this looks like a rock contact here and another over there." Her finger pointed to a heavy line near the center and one at the extreme right.

"Whazzat?"

"That's a place where two different kinds of rock come together. The markings on each side of the contacts indicate the kinds. It's hard to tell just what they are. Offhand, I'd venture the rock marked with crosses to be igneous, that with the straight marks to be sedimentary."

"Whoa up, you throwed me agin."

"Igneous rock was once melted, rock like granite or basalt. Sedimentary was deposited in layers, like sandstone or shale."

"Huh. Fancy lingo don't change factual. Them hills are all red granite, sandstone, and shale—no metal bearin' rocks in 'em." Rykoff gave a righteous scowl, then peered

70

at the map again, his curiosity piqued. "Yes. Well. How about these two picks I drew at the bottom, what do they signify? What do the marks 'A' and 'B' stand for? What does the arrow and the number 3210 mean?"

Jessie shrugged. "These, I'm afraid, were made up with their own meanings by whoever made up the map."

"Then what few facts you got won't help you greatly." Rykoff spoke half in question, half assertion. "The map is a bare-as—faced fakeroo. I never found sign of minin', past or present, and the minin' man I hired in reported I'd never see sign of silver or gold there, either. Nothing's there."

"Well, the Yaquis believed something was there, didn't they?"

"Apparently so, but I never found any relics of them, either. Back in the ol' days, though, they killed every poor soul who got in there. 'Peared to be guarding something they didn't want white men to see, but if they were, no one ever discovered what it was. Not in all the years since the country here and south of the Line began to fill up and the Yaquis were drove back down into the Sonora Mountains, where they still are. Just one of their damn fool superstitions, I reckon, or maybe just pure cussedness. The Yaquis never were an overly sociable lot and don't care to have outsiders hornin' in on them."

Jessie nodded. She, too, had heard outrageous stories of the jagged and gashed Big Bend region—stories of lost canyons carpeted with grass that was always green and watered by gushing springs, and shut in by palisaded walls where imprisoned herds of buffalo were still supposed to live. Stories of petrified forests with trees seven hundred feet long, of lost mines, and forgotten treasure hidden by the Conquistadores and those who came after them. Mostly just legends, but now and then with a grain of truth in them. She herself had seen pictures that no white man could ever decipher.

For the Big Bend was a land of tradition, where strange

71

characters had lived and yet lived. It was a country where strange things had happened and where anything might yet happen.

Jessie rode the night back to the Mashed-O. It seemed to her that she had put her ear to the pillow for only a second when it was time to get up again, and she was not far wrong. With pale pink smearing the eastern horizon, she saddled up and headed south down Mooneye Valley at a steady lope, not pushing her horse, but trying to conserve its energy for the long day of riding ahead.

Before long she reached the lower end of Mooneye Valley. While the sun rose brassy and waxen, she climbed the foothill cluster of rocks and arroyos that formed the south range of the Mashed-O spread. On through the Espantosa Hills she rode, scouting warily, their wild fastness befitting a hideout for desperadoes. Each gap, ridge, and pocket was a potential menace. Each tall mesa and beetling crag was a possible guntower for ruthless eyes. Even the sunlit calm within these enclosing elevations was a hushed yet vibrant warning to her suspicious ears.

And the more she rode, the more perplexing the situation seemed to her. The hills, so far as she could ascertain, were a desolate badlands of granite, sandstone, and shale. Occasionally she found some evidence of ancient volcanic action, but nowhere was there quartz or other gangue that would indicate the possible presence of precious metal. If such had been apparent, the probable answer to her quest would immediately have been present. Then it would have been logical to believe that somebody had discovered valuable ore deposits and consequently wanted possession of the land—somebody who either could not or would not pay the price to buy it. But search as she would, Jessie could find nothing to support the theory.

The sun was past its zenith, and heat waves were shimmering off the hills, when Jessie descended to the valley floor again. After a brief rest in a creekside grove of yew-leaf and sandbar willows, she rode into the murky gorge that channeled the stream through the hills. She had put off entering until she'd explored the hills above, but despite Zed Rykoff's insistence that it was impassable, she was resolved to check the gorge in an all-out effort to solve the puzzle.

The gorge was a solumn pit, for the stone walls towered so high that very little sunlight seeped down from the rimrock overhead. The stream, now a rushing torrent, chafed against its eroded banks and foamed up over jutting fangs of black stone. And for the first five miles, Jessie followed a narrow shelf of debris and rubble that hugged the base of the cliff. As far as she could determine, the gorge was as barren as the terrain above, lacking the slightest trace of silver or gold deposits.

Eventually she rounded a shoulder of stone and found corroboration of Zed Rykoff's statement. The shelf dwindled and the water washed the very base of the cliff. The gorge had straightened out at this point, and as far as she could see, the same condition prevailed. She urged her balky horse on through the swift current, the water close to the cliff wall comparatively shallow, though the bottom was treacherous with loose stones. She traversed the long straight stretch, rounded a shoulder of rock, and saw a similar stretch that extended for half a mile. A second shoulder disclosed yet another straight stretch.

With growing dismay, Jessie had to admit she was getting nowhere. Rykoff was right; the creek ran like this all the way through, and she was foolish to flounder on. She decided she'd go peer around the next bend, and if the course beyond didn't look any different, she'd turn back.

The stream curved gradually around a third jut of rock, then abruptly straightened once again. But this time the view was different, thanks to some prehistoric upheaval. Between buckled, striated walls of terra-cotta colored rock and heavier, darker volcanic rock, the creek swirled through a choppy, boulder-strewn patch of rapids. Edging the water line was another shelf, wider than the one which led to the first offset, but much shorter, ending a few hundred yards farther on.

Jessie rode across the shelf to the wall and, using her hunting knife, gouged out a lump of rock cliff for closer study. Although its minute details were hard to discern in the gloom, she took the chunk to be a meld of basalt and shale, with some jasper and iron oxides. Worthless. Disgusted, Jessie headed slowly along the shelf, mulling over the matter, her eyes roving about the dour, sinister spot in which she found herself.

She was nearing the end of the spit when she glimpsed a slender ledge that climbed the side of the gorge at an acute angle. It was not hidden, exactly, but blended indistinct with the cracked and cragged wall, easily overlooked from this angle and downright invisible from the creek. For a moment Jessie paused, wondering if her mount could scale the sharp ascent. Then setting her spurs, she prodded her horse clambering up the ledge.

The ledge became steeper, a series of switchbacks; soon Jessie was leading her horse on foot. The ledge crested and began to slope inward like the petal of a flower, then widened, and trailed off into a fold in the rock. Remounting at the crest, Jessie sat catching her breath, viewing the gorge and surrounding Espantosa Hills, and then rode on into the fold. She was soon following a deep rut or trench that kept plowing deeper and deeper, till at last it resembled a lane in stone and completely shut off the creek and far banks of the gorge. This singular lane twisted and writhed in accord with the terrain, but as she tried to keep mental track of her route, Jessie surmised the course was winding steadily north-westward.

Abruptly the trail ceased. Jessie emerged at the south end of a long, high bench of leveled slabstone, with the overhang of a cliff above her and a space of blue behind. Directly across at the north end, there appeared to be the mouth of another trail. Up front, the lip of the bench formed the edge of an abrupt chasm about sixty feet wide, and on the opposite side rose strange vermilion colored cliffs striped with bands of vivid scarlet.

Ground-reining her horse in shade by the trail, Jessie walked to the lip and peered down—and gave a sharp exclamation of astonishment. Some twenty-feet below the bench was a circular pool perhaps a dozen feet in diameter. Its edges were crusted with a lifeless-looking, varicolored substance that gave off a rainbow sheen in the sunlight that streamed from above. This sulfurous encrustation told Jessie that in eons past, when volcanic activity was manifest, the hollow had been a fumarole or small crater.

But it was the pool itself that held her attention. Motionless, gleaming silvery white, it filled the fumarole almost to its edge at the base of the walling cliffs. No ripple disturbed its placid surface. Smooth as a sheet of glass it lay, opaque, devoid of life. She picked up a fragment of stone and cast it into the pool, watching it strike the surface with a soft thud, and slowly sink as a sluggish ripple washed over it. No eddying ripples widened from where the shard broke the surface. What little was disturbed, though, reflected the sunlight like a shattered mirror, sending up blinding rays and beams.

Jessie glanced upward. Quickly she realized that the overhanging formation of the cliffs rendered the pool invisible from above, even if the ragged and broken crests were capable of being reached, which she doubted. The bench looked covered, too, though it stretched on for some half-score yards, to terminate in one of the peculiarly banded scarlet cliffs. Not far from the cliff face was a table of stone about eight feet in length by three in breadth, and supported by four pillars of stone that brought it about waist-high. And, peculiarly, it appeared to be formed in the shape of a Lorraine cross, with arms of stone protruding at right angles to its length at the head and foot.

Jessie started across the bench to take a gander at this oddity, and then at the other trail. But her eyes caught something else which quickened her pulse and turned her steps. In front of the other trail, fanning out from its mouth, spread a litter of cigarette butts. Jessie counted six on the ground nearby. They all appeared to have been quirlies, smoked short and mashed underfoot.

Glancing up the trail, Jessie listened intently but heard nothing. She saw another butt, though, a quirly like all the others, smoked short and mashed underfoot. A man of habits as well as a heavy smoker, Jessie reckoned, heading on to the stone table. She found the surface to be slightly concave, with holes bored in the stone at the center of the trough. The cross arms were notched. For a moment she was at a loss as to its significance—and then she stared at the darkly stained and blotched stone slab with sudden realization.

"So that's it!" she gasped, turning to glance at the strange, lifeless, gleaming pool as she thought: The Abode of the Mirror that Smokes. A lair for Texcatlipoca, who demanded sacrifices so the sun would cross the heavens each day. That was it, down in that hole, and this was the altar of sacrifice. The hands and feet of the victim were bound to those cross arms. . . .

Staring at the sinister, bloodstained slab, she envisaged the scenes that had been enacted here in this ghastly gash in the granite surface of the hills. She saw the dark-faced priest, his eyes burning with fanatical fire, in his reddened hand the gleaming obsidian knife of sacrifice. On the stone, bound hand and foot to the notched arms, the screaming victim. She saw the knife raised, the swift stroke, heard the agonized cry. Then the brawny acolytes bearing the still writhing body, food for the god, to the lip of the shelf, swinging it outward until it shot downward to the gleaming surface of the pool to strike with a sullen muffled thud. Then the slow sinking, the sluggish engulfing wave of the viscous liquid that strangled the last gasping scream, and the sacrifice vanishing forever.

Jessie was conscious of a sudden clammy moisture on her brow, a ringing in her ears. It was just an overwrought imagination, she knew, but just the same she didn't dawdle returning to her horse. Nor would she have been sorry to head back to the little shelf at the base of the gorge, with its noisy turbulence of the creek brawling past, so full of life and activity.

Instead she set off on the other trail. Again she entered a lane of stone, and again bore steadily northwestward, but the trails had their differences, too. This was a much longer trail, and much rougher due to the terrain. Sometimes its bed was wide, as much as fifteen, twenty feet, then unexpectedly it would narrow until hazardous for legs with a horse's bulging sides squeezing the cliff walls. Jessie lost count of the times she'd had to dismount, lead her horse, mount again.

Eventually the trail came to an end. Dipping her hat against the sunset glare, Jessie rode out across a slope and wondered where'n hell she was. She knew where she was going—down. She sure wouldn't be going up; the ridgelines and bare elevations up around her would've made a mountain goat blanch. Well, naturally whoever built the trails hadn't wanted just everybody dropping in.

That left the slope, which funneled steeply through a shadowed ravine. Working her way down, Jessie noticed that the slope was growing matted with nettles, briers, and thistles, increasingly so, until they were spilling down and clogging the floor of the ravine. She let her horse set its own pace, and concentrated on detecting anything amiss. The only thing amiss, however, seemed to be the vegetation, becoming a solid tangle of thorns all around and ahead of her.

Jessie was thinking to backtrack and search for an easier route, when she became aware that her horse, on its own, had been slowly nosing through the blockage on a carefully disguised path. She stopped to inspect the surrounding briers and vines which appeared, even at a very short distance, to securely prevent any passage. Leaning over, she saw that the dense growth had been slyly pruned, the stickers and thorns clipped off, so that actually a rider could slip through unharmed, the underbrush springing shut behind like a gate in a fence.

Gradually the thorns and thistles died away. Jessie passed into a region of jumbled foothills spiked with acadia and agaves, the rugged terrain dulling with encroaching dusk, blurring over and filling in with shadows, when at length she came upon a wagon road. Cutting north on it, she had ridden for perhaps a mile when the clatter of hooves on stone warned her that someone was coming.

Coming fast. And furious.

For a moment the galloping horseman was silhouetted cresting a sag. Too far and too dark to actually see any detail, though some slight mannerism seemed familiar to Jessie. Still, there was a time to fight and a time to run, but this was not the time, nor the place, and her horse was too tired to run.

So just to be prudent, Jessie eased off-trail into a shouldering bosque of honey mesquite. Snubbing her horse close, she clapped her hat over its nostrils. The rider loomed suddenly, a charging silhouette against the night sky. So close at that instant she could hear the labored breathing of his horse, the ring of irons.

Her fingers closed on the butt of her pistol—finger caressed the chilly metal of the trigger.

★

Chapter 6

On the day before, Ki returned to consciousness with cool, hardpacked dirt pressing against his cheek. He lay there for a long time, confused and bewildered, wondering dully why there should be dirt under his face. He stirred a little and opened his eyes.

A large, indistinct bulky object loomed nearby. Ki could see he was lying in a long, low room, and nearby a heavyset Mexican was slouched at a table, sucking on a toothpick. Thin shafts of sunlight angled through a pair of iron-barred, slotlike window ports, one on each sidewall. Beyond their meager strips of illumination the room disappeared in ghostly gloom.

Ki's head ached and it hurt him to move. His arms were lashed tightly behind him although his legs were free. He lay still awhile and the pain subsided. Finally he spoke to the man at the table.

"Where am I, amigo?"

"Does it matter, gringo? You are the prisoner of Luiz Zugate—*eso es todo*, that's all." Shrugging, the Mexican rose and strode across to a distant door. He knocked; someone outside unlatched the door and he stepped through, the door locking closed behind him.

Quietly Ki tested the ropes binding him. They were tight and well-knotted—but not tight or knotted enough. A slight, humorless smile creased his mouth as he twisted and flexed his wrists, sensing the weak points. His captors, putting their faith in the ropes restraining him, would be less watchful and cautious.

By now his eyes had become adjusted to the darkness. The object near him became a heavy, crude cart with the high wooden wheels that probably shrieked noisily every time it moved. A skeleton, with a grinning skull, rode in the plank seat. Its bony hands held a drawn bow, the arrow aimed to the floor somewhere between Ki and the table. Peering closely, Ki discerned that the skeleton was not genuine, but had been carved with wood, and in broad daylight probably looked quite crude. But in the half-darkness it changed into a sinister, brooding figure filled with strange silent menace.

This, Ki realized, had to be a chapel of the Penitentes, no doubt long since abandoned. He remembered the times he had seen processions of that strange sect of *flagelentes* whipping themselves until the blood ran down their backs, singing their weird songs and pulling replicas of the death cart that loomed so close beside him. The members were normally peaceful but deadly when anyone interfered with their rites. This place had one time been used by them and now, evidently, had been taken over by Luiz Zugate and his gang.

That was not the entire answer, Ki learned moments later, when the door opened and another man stepped inside. Only his dark silhouette was visible at first, arm extended, gripping a Colt revolver.

"Hello, Starbucker."

It was an American voice. Not the same voice he'd overheard at the shack, but it was familiar. From far back. Ki couldn't remember where, until the man moved within the glow of lamplight. He wore grubby range garb, with an eagle feather stuck in the brim of a low-crowned sombrero. His face was dead white, with black stubble on his chin, bloodless lips, and a latent threat in his fierce gray eyes. It was Brazos Chaldeen, a rustler from east central Texas who'd more than once plagued the Circle Star.

"Why, hello Chaldeen."

Chaldeen grinned with a twist of his hard slashed mouth. "I thought you'd remember me, Ki. All you ever forget are the faces of dead men."

Ki chuckled low, none too pleasantly. "You used to boss a fair-sized bunch, Chaldeen. How come you joined the ranks of these Mexican border scum?"

"I ain't that big a idjit, Ki. We have, er, arrangements 'tween us, and since my ranch was handy—"

"Your ranch?"

"The Gridiron. They brung you here for safe-keepin', a damnfool risk and I told 'em so. But that's their deal, I ain't party to it. Don't get no hopes up. When Juan reported you come to, I thought I'd come by to say howdy-do, but I ain't helpin' you out neither." Chaldeen still held the gun, not cocked, just with his thumb hooked over the hammer. "You're the one who set the deadfall in Mooneye Canyon last night, weren't you?"

"You think if I'd set it, you'd even be here?"

Chaldeen laughed. "Maybe so, but you're the one with brains to trail us. You're not like Zugate. He swaggers and beats his chest, and you just sit with your mouth shut. But not this time." He jiggled the gun muzzle. "Okay, Ki, open up. What're you doing here?"

"Zugate must've told you. I was following him."

"Reckoning he'd lead you to me?"

"To hell with you. I'm after bigger game."

"Big as Luiz Zugate?"

"I don't give a particular damn about him and his bug-crawling bandidos, any more than I do about you. You're forgotten, Chaldeen, and you'll remain forgotten as long as you stay clear of Starbuck interests. But don't cross our line again, or you'll wind up on the end of a riata cravat. Now, quit acting stupid and put up the gun."

Chaldeen heard Ki with an off-center grin twisting his thin, predatory face. "Well, by damn! I never thought I'd be talked into anything by a Starbucker." He slid the gun back in its holster.

"I'll keep my promise, " Ki said softly. "Just like I always do."

"Uh-huh, and that about the riata cravat, too. I'll lay dollars to pesos you'd tie the knot yourself."

"No. I think I'd bury you right where I had to kill you. You're not the kind that gives up alive." Then Ki asked, "Who's El Cascabel?"

"Quien sabe?"

"You mean you ride with him and don't know who he is?"

"I mean I don't know what you're talking about."

"Of course. But Zugate does. He knows El Cascabel had to be behind your raid last night, trying to pull a fast one by taking the cattle for himself."

"You *are* sharp, aren't you? Damn sharp. Well, listen, I got places to go, but if you're still here in a day or two, I'll drop by again. Meanwhile, there'll be a little of everybody around. Don't let 'em catch you getting too sharp, 'cause they're just the boys to dummy you flat with forty-fours."

Chaldeen left Ki then. The Mexican guard, waiting outside, entered and resumed his seat at the table.

Ki relaxed, feeling a bit more confident, and continued pressuring the ropes lightly with his wrists. But he made no overt move to break loose. He was still weak, woozy, hurting where the bullet had creased the blood-encrusted side of his head. His vest had been taken, and with it his

82

weapons. Sounds of men constantly echoed through the window ports, indicating that even if he overpowered this gent, he'd probably not get beyond the locked door. So for now Ki was willing to play the prisoner, to regain his strength and wait for an opportunity, and perhaps learn why he was being kept alive. To be questioned, he supposed, though he sensed there was more to it than that. . . .

Along about sunset the guard was replaced by a leaner, taller Mexican of Indian blood. Possibly of the Tarahumara, Ki guessed, from western Chihuahua. Wherever the man was from, he plainly didn't like where he was now. The darker it grew, and the later it grew, and the quieter it grew outside, the greater perturbed he grew.

Ki let the man stew, dozing off and on through the night. He awoke alert when the man went outside to piss, and noted he let himself out the door. And Ki awoke alert during the early morning hours, sensing it was in that predawn stillness between three and five A.M., when sleep is the soundest and those awake are at their most relaxed. Except for the increasingly nervous guard.

Ki spoke in a soft hissing voice. "Señor . . . señor . . ."

The man jerked and his revolver glinted as he swung, bearing aim. Ki held his breath; the man was frightened and might pull the trigger. But in a moment the man regained control over his shaky nerves. "*Por Dios*, what a scare."

"Señor, water . . ."

"*Deja de ladrar*—stop yapping." The man scowled threateningly at Ki and settled back down in the chair. But he kept casting glances out into the shadows as though terribly anxious about something unseen.

By now Ki understood the man's trepidations. Part Indian, the Mexican knew of the Penitentes and feared their hidden power. "The place of the Penitentes," he murmured darkly. "It is *muy malo* to enter this place."

The Mexican shuddered. "It is not to speak, hombre. Luiz Zugate, he has no fear of the dead ones."

"That's bad for him," Ki answered. "The ghosts will return. This is their holy place, and you know it. They will be angry, and you know it."

The Mexican groaned and crossed himself. His eyes darted swiftly into the shadows. "Hombre, I have told Luiz those things. But he does not listen. I, Fabien Duron, have seen what these old ones do when they are angered. I have heard their curses."

"Luiz Zugate laughs at the devils," Ki declared, "and the devils will strike. Not only him, señor, but at us all. You and me—at everyone who has defiled the chapel."

Fabien Duron trembled. Shakily he rolled a cigarette as Ki edged closer to the *carreta muerta*. Ki could almost touch it with his foot . . . just another inch . . . Duron turned to face him and he froze.

"Hombre, you are *simpático*. You savvy these old ones. It is sad I must hold you so." The man glanced around the shadows again, and Ki edged over till his foot touched the long tongue. Carefully he worked his toe under the shaft. His eyes watched the man, gauging his move as his muscles grew taut. . . .

Suddenly the death cart creaked as Ki raised the shaft with his foot. Fabien Duron jumped, frightened eyes fastening in horror on the slowly tipping cart. The shaft fell back with a crash. The skeleton on the seat shook and trembled, appearing in the gloom to raise the bow as if about to shoot.

With a squall of terror, the Mexican sprang from the table and leaped for the door. Ki heard the man sob as he groped frantically for the catch, finally wrenching the door open and disappearing out into the night.

Immediately Ki started working on his bonds. He tugged and twisted at the ropes until he worked a hand free, burning the skin. In another moment he was loose and rubbing his wrists to restore circulation, heading warily for the doorway. He had no idea if his guard would recover from his fright or go rousting others. Cautiously he peered outside.

The decrepit adobe chapel sat on a shallow rise, flanked by four crumbling huts. It overlooked the Gridiron ranchstead below, consisting of an elongated, tarpaper-roofed cabin, some brush-covered ramadas, and an oversized pole corral. Also down there was the chapel's original stone well, its water no doubt the reason Chaldeen broke taboo to squat on sacred ground.

Even from this distance the Gridiron appeared shabby and furtive. Ki saw horses in the corral but no sign of men, though they could be sacked out in the cabin or ramadas, or perhaps in the seemingly abandoned huts closeby. Far away he could glimpse a silent glow against the dark horizon, and realized that must be Quevidas yonder. Accordingly it meant he was on the north shore of the Rio, toward the western end of Boquillas Canyon, he estimated roughly, near Tornillo Creek.

Nothing stirred. Only the normal nocturnal sounds came to his ears.

Breathing easier, Ki was about to step outside when he heard something rustle, and he dipped back into the shadows of the door. The sound approached, a hesitant almost fearful slither of huaraches, and now he could make out the murky figure of the guard, Fabien Duron.

Hastily Ki glanced around for some weapon, not needing any to kill, but wanting one to intimidate the guard. He could only find a short, chunky stick of wood. Without a sound, Ki grabbed his makeshift club and waited tensely.

Duron came closer, the silence of the chapel evidently giving him courage. At last, breathing raggedly, he paused outside the door and poked his head in. The lamp shed too little light for him to see if his prisoner was still there or not. Apprehensively he stepped into the chapel, pointing his revolver.

Ki shoved his stick in the small of the man's back. "Reach, amigo, or you'll be a ghost yourself."

Gasping convulsively, the guard shot his hands above his head.

Ki snatched the pistol from Duron's fingers and exchanged it for the wood stick. "Over to the table, amigo, where I can see you better."

The guard obeyed, and with the gun muzzle in his ribs, meekly turned up the lamp a notch. As the light flared, Ki could see more clearly the high cheekbones and deep coppery color that disclosed the Indian in Duron's scared face. He stepped away a pace, revolver still leveled.

"Now, answer me. Who's your *jefe*, your chief?"

"Luiz Zugate, as surely you—"

"Who is the chief behind Zugate?"

Duron hesitated, licked his lips, and cast a fearful look at the pistol. "Felipe Murillo, señor. He take most the pesos when the cattle are sold."

But Ki was recalling the mysterious rider who had met Luiz Zugate and talked like an American. The cantina owner might direct Zugate or serve as a go-between, but someone was behind Felipe Murillo. "No, there's a gringo. He comes to see Murillo and Zugate and Brazos Chaldeen, too. Who's the gringo?"

Duron looked genuinely surprised. "I do not know such an hombre, señor. Luiz Zugate and Felipe Murillo, they are the ones who truly lead us."

Ki searched the guard's face by the flickering lampglow. He had to admit Fabien Duron thought he was telling the truth; it was written in the frightened lines of his simple features. Disappointed, Ki tried another tack.

"What're they up to? What're their plans?"

"Señor, I know nothing. Nobody tells me—"

"Too bad." Ki thumbed back the gunhammer.

"*M-madre de Dios!*" Duron babbled, ogling the pistol. "T-there is talk, señor, talk of hitting Fortuna Mine tomorrow night. S-si, and while you're our prisoner, to—"

A volley of gunshots blasted simultaneously from the doorway, aimed carefully. One slug ripped Duron's throat to shreds, as though from an inner explosion; two more pounded into his upper chest; half the crown of his head went off with another. He fell out of the chair in jerky spasms, withering terribly, dead before he landed on the floor.

Whirling in a crouch, Ki brought the pistol to bear—

"Fire," a voice snapped, "and we'll blow your fuckin' brains out!"

Confronting Ki, seven men loomed inside the doorway with drawn revolvers, four of which were smoking. Front and center stood the one who spoke, Felipe Murillo. He was sided by two in bandido garb, while the others grouping around him were range-clad, equally dirty and sweat-streaked, their expressions bleary and nasty mean. Obviously the huts weren't as abandoned as they'd seemed.

Slowly, gingerly, Ki placed his weapon on the ground.

"Ver' well," Murillo said. "Take him, *muchachos*, tie him tight. Show this smart turd don' wriggle loose again."

The six henchmen moved in with more relish than caution, while Murillo held Ki at bay with his finger tight around the trigger. They piled on him, clamping his arms. Ki jerked and whipsawed, shaking off one armlock, then catching and twisting the other, causing a bandido to shriek as muscles and tendons were wrenched painfully. A pistol butt struck the back of his head, then another, hammering hard, driving Ki down to his knees. He struggled to rise, both arms gripped tightly again by men who hung on and tried to keep him down. Their pistols pounded, pounded, and already suffering the effects of a concussion, Ki felt himself sinking, almost passing out.

"Don't kill him!" Murillo ordered. "He is worth something alive!"

Gritting his teeth against the brutal pistol-whipping, Ki fought his way to his feet again, using fists, elbows, teeth, knees, his entire body as a weapon. But it was useless. He reeled, vision blurring, blinding pain seeming to shatter his skull as their guns clubbed his head with stunning force, and he slumped unconscious to the floor. . . .

Gradually his senses returned, along with a ferocious headache worse than before. Ki lay on his side in the dirt again, but now he found himself trussed by the ankles as well as wrists, and shackled with some old handcuffs to the wheelrim of the cart. Nobody was guarding him, though; evidently Murillo had more confidence in the bonds keeping Ki here than in his men keeping their mouths shut.

For a while Ki merely sat resting, and then he began to free himself. Focusing his concentration on the task, he purposely dislocated the bones of his wrists, then his hands, even his nimble fingers. Then, by merely twisting and stretching his ligaments and muscles, he slowly wormed his limp, formless flesh through the encoiling rope and the steel cuffs. The rope dropped empty to the floor behind his back; the cuffs dangled by their chain from the wheel.

Snapping his bones back into place, Ki quickly unknotted the rope around his ankles. He stood, stretching his cramped muscles, and started to prowl the gloomy chapel. The lamp had broken, but daylight once again pierced the window ports, illuminating weakly. Duron was a hideously gory sight, yet Ki could do nothing about the corpse without tipping off that he'd gotten free. His search proved futile; there was no way out except through the door, and no way to get through the door until it was unbarred.

Ki settled back where he'd lain. Sooner or later someone had to come in, or he would be led outside. Given a split-second's chance, he would take full advantage of it. Meanwhile he savored the respite, suspecting he might not have another opportunity for a long time afterward . . . if not for the rest of his life, R.I.P. . . .

Slowly the sun arced across the sky, roasting the day. Around the chapel remained stifling quiet, while intermittently sounds of men and horses drifted up from the ranch.

When finally the sun was rimming the Chisos Mountains, its slanting rays burnishing the western exposure of the chapel, Ki heard a passel of riders gathering below, then charge off in a thunderous drumming of hooves. Silence followed, a stillness as if the Gridiron lay deserted.

Fifteen, twenty minutes later came the galloping ring of horses' irons on stony ground. They were only a few, Ki perceived, the beat of irons growing louder. As the returning horsemen topped the rise and reined up at the chapel, he looped rope around his ankles and flattened against the wheelrim, his arms behind him like they were still bound and cuffed. The latch rattled, the bolt clanked, the door swung open on squeaky iron hinges.

Six men crowded in, the six who'd sided with Murillo.

"Hell, looky there," one of the gringo gunhands sneered. "He'd be up, I said, didn't I?"

"Righ', Tully," another hooted, "Chinks got cast-iron skulls."

Lantern-jawed, slot-eyed, grinning as the others sniggered, Tully strutted bowlegged across and stood akimbo over Ki. "The boss is sending a note to your gal, boy," he taunted, nudging Ki with the toe of his boot. "If'n she wants you back, she's better come collect you. You're bait, boy, live bait." With a snarl, he kicked Ki viciously in the gut.

Ki, anticipating, employed a *tandem* technique to ready his abdominal muscles, and absorbed the kick without harm or pain. Straightening slightly, arms still behind him, he said coldly, "Try that again, and I'll kill you."

Tully laughed derisively. "You nervy asshole! We've got a few scores to square on our own, and th' way we see it, we got our chance now." Drawing his revolver, Tully swung a pistol-whipping blow with his right hand while punching with his left, adding, "An' nobody's told us how 'live you've gotta be!"

Ki killed him.

Ducking, Ki gripped the revolver and wrenched it back,

breaking Tully's trigger finger with a spasmodic firing of one shot. Ignoring the bullet slamming upward into the chapel roof, Ki used his other arm to block the fist aiming for his midriff, then rammed the heel of his palm in a *teisho* blow to Tully's nose, driving shards of broken cartilage up into his brain. Tully died on his feet.

Enraged, the other five men stormed Ki, bent on revenge. Ki dropped the nearest man with a back-knuckled "ram's head" jab between the eyes. Without turning, without apparently seeing his target, he stabbed the second with a left-handed thumb-and-forefinger thrust to the larynx, crushing the man's windpipe, crumpling him instantly to the ground. Meanwhile, he stopped the man tackling from the rear with a sideways snap-kick; clutching his hemmorhaging solar plexus, the man sank lifeless to his knees. But the fourth man managed to come in butting from the other side, knocking Ki just enough off balance so he could gouge his knee in the small of Ki's back and apply a full nelson.

"Got him! Kill the fucker!"

"You betcha!" The fifth man lunged, brandishing a .44 S. & W. revolver in one hand, and a groove-bladed skinning knife in the other.

Using the man behind him for support, Ki bunched his legs in a flying upward thrust, his heels catching the fifth man square in the balls. The man doubled up, uttering short croaks of agony and confusion, almost neutering himself as he pawed at his crotch with weapon-laden hands.

Then, planting his feet firmly on the floor again, Ki simply backed up. The man behind him, who had both arms and one foot engaged in the lock he had on Ki, was thrown immediately off balance, and had to remove the knee he'd put in the small of Ki's back, to keep from falling. So Ki just relaxed and bent his knees and dropped out from under the full nelson, turning as he did so to deliver a *yoko-hija-ate* sideways elbow smash, caving in

90

the man's ribs and stopping his heart. The fifth man went down.

The fifth but not the last. It had taken only a moment to deal with him, but that moment had allowed the fourth man to recover somewhat. Enough to rear up holding his pistol, aiming point-blank at Ki through watering eyes. Ki kicked in the side of his head, crushing the temple bone like an eggshell.

After snatching up the man's revolver and skinning knife, Ki raced out of the chapel, locked the door, and flung away the big iron key. He saw no sign of his horse among the few mustangs in the corral, but he could hear querulous, alarmed shouts rising from the cabin. So much for hopes of snooping around down there. Glancing over the six scruffy mounts tied at the chapel hitchpost, Ki swung aboard a hock-scarred, surly brute of a mustang, noting the rifle in the saddle scabbard. As they were leaving, whoever was in the cabin ran out and let rip with a double-barreled 12-gauge shotgun, inspiring the mustang with spirited gusto. They made tracks at a flat-out gallop.

As the sun burned the day to ashen dusk, Ki rode the hills westward, more or less, aiming to cut north before he hit Tornillo Creek. He'd have druther headed the opposite way—to Quevidas, in need of a cleanup; or simply back to the Mashed-O. Yet Fabien Duron had blurted something about a raid tonight on the Fortuna Mine. Besides, eastward hoved the twisted badlands that bordered the Boquillas, and Ki couldn't risk getting lost at this stage of the game.

Well, neither could he afford running into Zugate's bandido horde at this point. Fortunately they weren't on the lookout for him, at least not yet. Ki doubted, too, that Felipe Murillo would waste time gathering men to recapture him. That could change once they busted in the chapel door and saw the bodies, but hopefully by then it'd be too late.

More troubling to Ki was the unknown, unpredictable El Cascabel, for there was no telling what he would do. In turn, though, another problem had become clearer, his pinch at the chapel was not an entire loss. Brazos Chaldeen played a part in this puzzle, maybe an important part, but he played it through coercion. Come the showdown, Ki sensed a chance that the Gridiron might desert the mysterious bossman who held Chaldeen under his thumb.

Ki wouldn't want to bet his life on it, though.

★

Chapter 7

Palming her pistol, Jessica Starbuck stood breathless with her horse in the mesquite's half concealment, watching the night-shrouded rider's looming approach. Despite her rigid silence, the rider seemed to sense a hidden presence, and hesitated, peering around with a revolver in hand. She caught a glimpse of his face and nearly burst out laughing in relief. It was Ki.

Hailing him, Jessie stepped out to trailside. "What're you doing here?" she asked as he pulled up, then got a closer look. "My god, what happened to you?"

"I'm all right. I'm going to the Fortuna Mine," Ki answered, "if I can find it. You haven't got anything to eat, have you?"

"Leftovers." She dug out two roast beef sandwiches, wrapped in oily paper, from her saddlebags. Roast beef sandwiches were saloon staples; before leaving the Paydirt Bar, Jessie had bought a half-dozen from Sam, at a nickle apiece. "I wouldn't mind to visit Fortuna, myself," she said thoughtfully, mounting her grulla. "Let's compare happenings on the way."

Continuing up the wagon road, Ki devoured the sandwiches and listened to Jessie recount her experiences with his characteristic gravity. Jessie was less reserved as he related his findings to her.

"The bastard!" she snapped when Ki finished. "I'm sure you're right, Ki. Whoever's behind all this mess is American and deviously shrewd. Holding you hostage isn't the kind of stunt pulled by a rustler like Brazos Chaldeen, or his alias, the Pecos Kid. Sending me a ransom demand wouldn't be the work of bandidos, either."

"No matter what deal El Cascabel set up, though, I doubt he would've kept it. We would've found out, just like Zugate found out about the Mashed-O raid, that the sidewinder can't be trusted," Ki said. "It would've been a trap."

Jessie nodded. "He probably figured I'd risk it anyhow, and he'd do away with us both. But . . . for all that trouble, what did he expect to gain? How could that ensure him the valley . . . ?" She paused, eyes narrowing, pondering. "Ki, perhaps the gunman who bragged his boss was sending a note to 'your gal' wasn't referring to me, but to Prudence. Maybe you were bait to lure her."

"Good point. I think maybe we should head straight back to the ranch, soon as we check the mine. . . ."

Their knowledge of the immediate country was scant, but Jessie had learned back in Ingot last night the general location of Big Nick Tualatin's Fortuna Mine. And they were fairly certain where they were now. They each had headed east until intercepting this trail, which for all practical purposes was the only north-south route through the Big Bend—the same wagon road they had originally taken to Ingot, and then to the cutoff to the Mashed-O. Now they were south of the cutoff, where the road went down along Tornillo Creek to the Rio and beyond into Mexico.

Night had smoothed the terrain to a textured ebony as infinite as the blackened sky by the time they approached the junction of a secondary trail that angled in from the left. Turning onto it, they followed the deep ruts gouged by heavy ore wagons, crossing a crude wooden bridge over Tornillo creek, and climbed west by north through foothills up into the Rosillos Mountains.

Occasionally they would spot the distant campfire of a miner's digs. But otherwise they had only a diamond spray of stars to view, and the faintest hint of where in a few days the new moon would form. After quite a stretch, they began flanking the narrow, sawtooth cut of a feeder stream, though bouldered outcroppings and scrub-dotted slopes in between hid the noisy whitewater flow from sight. The trail wound on through the rockribbed hills, campfires growing fewer, then seeming to die out altogether. Eventually they came to the site of the Fortuna Mine. It was just beyond the next curve, they realized, glimpsing the peaked roofline of its shafthouse jutting above the bend's hilly shoulder, sharp-etched against the starry night sky.

Jessie reined in. "I don't hear anything or see any light ahead."

"We might be too early or too late, or just plain bum steered and wrong," Ki responded, scanning the shoulder. "But let's not take a chance."

Urging his horse off-trail, Ki located a murky pocket of bluewood and guayacan, and beckoned for Jessie to follow. Ground-tying their mounts in the shelter, they hiked up the rocky bank to the rim of the shoulder, then crossed to peer down the opposite side, into a darksome canyon. Heaps of mine tailings made a scar on the slope below. The shafthouse marked the opening of Big Nick Tualatin's claim, which they understood was only a couple of years old; yet already the roof and walls of lanceleaf cottonwood showed heavy weathering.

Ki shrugged. "I have to agree, Jessie. The mine sounds deserted."

As if on cue, a high-pitched scream of agony echoed from the shafthouse—the cry of a man in mortal suffering.

They started down the steep slope, angling from boulder to boulder, trying not to launch noisily tumbling rocks or gravel slides. Midway down they had to follow a ledge to the leftward, to avoid jumping over a short cliff. In doing so, they swung in view of rubble dumped outside a tunnel mouth in the canyon wall, some fifty yards from the shafthouse. They also could see a group of saddle horses tied to the wooden supports of a big blasting screen, erected by miners to protect the shafthouse from flying debris when they set off charges in the mountain side.

Reaching the base of the slope, they slipped through the shadows to the the shafthouse. On one side were a few steps leading to a ground floor door, and on the other was a single window that had been covered by a horseblanket. Approaching, they could hear muffled activity, but couldn't look in until they were almost pressing their noses against the window, peering through a thin sliver where the hem of the blanket brushed the lower sill.

Inside was lantern-lit, showing a grisly scene. A handful of sombreroed, hairy-jawed men grouped about the kerosene lantern, which hung on a nail driven in a thick beam supporting the windlass drum of the mineshaft elevator. Across the yawning shaft, Luiz Zugate leaned against a massive iron safe, its double doors locked, a cardboard sign dangling by a string from its combination knob:

WARNING!

THIS SAFE FULL OF EXPLOSIVES

BLOW OPEN AT YOUR OWN PERIL!

W.D.

Three of the bandidos held frayed and blood-stained ropes, with knots at the ends. They all were staring upward at a swaying figure, stripped to his waist, hanging over the open mineshaft from a rope tied to a crossbeam above.

"Tell me the combination numbers, *idiota*, or do we have to lash the meat off your bones?" Zugate was snarling. "I tire of your stallings!"

Nausea clutched Jessie and Ki as the swinging victim turned slowly like a carcass of beef. It was Wade Duval, the half-naked office manager suspended by his wrists, his muscle-corded torso and arms lacerated with bloody, blue-green welts from the torture he had endured. His jaws were clamped tight, his eyes misted cups in their sockets, lackluster with torment.

"You can whup me to death," Duval croaked feebly. "I ain't got a prayer, nohow. 'Least I'll pass out knowin' you never got your swag. Try crackin' the safe, and y'all meet me in hell, damn yuh!"

Jessie winced guiltily; after all, it'd been her idea to rig the safe with blasting powder. She gripped her pistol, burning as she saw the bandidos drive their knotted ropes into Duval's bare flesh, seething as she heard his agonized groans. Ki was chafing to strike as well, yet they both knew that to force a premature showdown would seal Wade Duval's doom. Zugate and his men had to be taken all at once by surprise. The first thing they would do, if any of them suspected or survived a sneak attack, would be to murder Duval and drop his corpse down the mineshaft.

"Give him a few more licks," Zugate ordered. "If a rope will not loosen his tongue, we will get a chunk of wire cable off the windlass drum. Or maybe a bit of halter chain."

"I ain't spilling," Duval muttered, grimacing. "I wouldn't if I could, but I can't rec'lect that combination nohow, the way my noggin's twirling."

With a guttural curse, Zugate snatched a knotted rope

away from one of his bandidos and began thrashing Duval, flailing in a fit of rage. Duval never uttered another sound, but suddenly, silently fell limp, head drooping on his chest, body twisting slackly from the ropes above the shaft.

For a horrified moment Jessie feared Duval had died as a result of his beatings. Then she saw the man's ribs lifting and falling.

"The *cretino* has conked out!" Zugate raged, flinging the rope aside. "Esteban, go down to the stream here and fetch a bucket of water to douse him with. Andale!"

Their victim unconscious for the time being, Zugate and the other bandidos sat down on the shaft combing and began rolling cigarettes. The bandido named Esteban scrounged around bellyaching, found a battered coal skuttle to use as a pail, and picked up a shotgun on his way out of the shafthouse.

Flattening their backs against the shafthouse wall, Jessie and Ki tensed as the bandido passed within a dozen feet, heading for the yonder stream. They exchanged glances, tempted to waylay him and whittle the odds. Problem was, the ground was layered with pebbly gravel, the kind the crunches underfoot no matter how softly one treads. Even Ki in his rope-soled slippers doubted he could sneak close enough for a silent attack and still catch the man off-guard. If discovered, the resulting uproar would alert Zugate and crew—exit bandidos; good-bye Duval.

However, as they watched the bandido trudging by the rubbled mouth of the tunnel, a notion occurred to Jessie. "Ki," she whispered, "that tunnel over there may well be a crosscut, connecting with the main shaft about, oh, thirty feet below floor level."

"Below Wade Duval," Ki amended, nodding. "Worth a look."

When the bandido had plodded out of range, they stole across the slope to the tunnel entrance. Ducking inside the dark maw, they groped blindly along the subterranean passage, burrowing through inky blackness with unseen critters scuttling and fluttering out of their path. The tunnel curved leftward at an oblique angle and, rounding the elbow bend, they saw a faint wash of light at its end. Lantern light, shafting down from the windlass house above ground.

The light enabled them to pick their way through a forest of rough-hewn shoring timbers, rock chips, muck and debris. A few minutes later they reached the brink of the main vertical shaft. Gripping support timbers, Jessie and Ki leaned out over the edge, peering upward.

Thirty feet overhead they saw the foreshortened body of Wade Duval, twisting slowly by his wrists. The lantern glow silhouetted Luiz Zugate and most of his men, lounging on the windlass combing, their legs dangling over the edge of the shaft while they puffed cigarettes.

The shaft below plunged to unfathomable depths. Across, some ten feet away, was the continuation of the crosscut, which had followed a vein of silver ore. On both sides of the shaft were heavy snubbing timbers, used to lash down the elevator deck when halting to load ore from the crosscut. The only sign of the elevator were vertical cables vanishing into the abyss, their wire strands already appearing frayed and corroded.

An idea crystalized full-born in Ki's mind.

He motioned to Jessie, and they retraced their steps back to the tunnel entrance. Huddling outside, no longer in danger of their voices carrying, he spoke swiftly, outlining his plan. She eyed him askance, flabbergasted.

"Ki, that is the craziest scheme I've ever heard tell."

"You want to give it a try, or don't you?"

Jessie smiled. "We've got to work fast, before Wade Duval regains consciousness and they start whipping him again."

Quickly yet quietly, they went over where the bandidos' mustangs were tied to the large blasting net. Rolls of thick wire mesh lay about, used by miners when and wherever screening was needed from explosions. Picking up two of the rolls, they paused long enough to remove four coiled lariats from the saddles of the horses, then returned to the tunnel and worked back to the main shaft.

None of the bandidos were visible, but Jessie and Ki could hear gruffly muttered voices resonating down the shaft. By dim rays of lantern light, they studied the snubbing timbers on the other side of the shaft, and the matching posts set in the tunnel floor where they stood. Shaking out loops in two of the lariats, they lassoed both snubbing posts opposite, then drew their ropes taut, dallying them around handy posts and knotting them securely. They did the same thing with the other two ropes, crisscrossing them to form a sort of rope platform spanning the vertical shaft.

Then, without so much as a whisper between them, they unrolled the screen. By sliding it out over the horizontal ropes, they were able to push the wire mesh across to the opposite mouth of the crosscut. That done, they drew their knives and cut off the slack ends of the four lariats. Chopping the hard-twist manilla lass'-ropes into foot-long sections, they proceeded to lash down the edges of the wire netting to the supporting ropes, crawling on all fours out on the double layer of metal screen.

Leery about this plan to begin with, Jessie was gratified to find that the makeshift platform supported the weight of them both. Reaching the other side of the tunnel, she and Ki used up the remainder of their rope in tying the screen platform to the elevator cables, and to the two crisscrossing lariats that formed an X from corner to corner. On their way back she watched with bated breath as Ki walked upright, testing the impromptu platform. It sagged springily, but was amply strong to support them.

Ki nodded, silently satisfied as they withdrew into the crosscut passage. When it was safe to talk, he murmered, ''That wire screen is tough enough to hold flying rocks and stuff from blastings, and the lariats won't break when

100

a ton of steer hits the dead end of a daubed reata. So I reckon it'll hold Wade Duval and me.''

"Good luck," she whispered. "I'll be waiting."

Hastening out of the tunnel, Ki padded back across to the shafthouse. As he peered through the window again, he witnessed Wade Duval recovering consciousness, aided by Luiz Zugate throwing a skuttle-full of water over his half-naked body.

"I give you one las' chance," Zugate warned Duval, tossing the skuttle at Esteban. "If you don' talk this time, we won' whip you no more. We try some other games. Shaving the soles off your feet, or roasting splinters under your skin."

"I'll take the—numbers with me," Duval gasped convulsively. "Go on—go do your damndest. I'll see you muckers to the devil first!''

Ki waited to hear no more. Skirting the wall of the shafthouse, he drew his borrowed revolver as he reached the front door and climbed up on the sloping ramp which led to the windlass platform. Halting in the threshold, he paused a second to memorize the positions of the bandidos. All had their backs to him, and were staring vulturously as Luiz Zugate drew back his arm to begin rawhiding Wade Duval again with a crimson-smeared, knotted rope.

Hoping the S. & W. .44 would fire generally where he pointed it, Ki took a careful bead on the lantern which hung from the support beam. The revolver roared deafeningly and recoiled against the heel of Ki's hand. Glass jangled as the bullet smashed the lamp, and the shafthouse was plunged into total darkness.

Gliding forward and to the left, Ki skirted the windlass and came to a halt alongside the shaft combing, opposite where the bandidos were frozen, for the moment, in confused shock. Then bedlam burst loose, accompanied by the slog of boots and the scrape of guns leaving leather as they lunged for the shelter of the corners, convinced that they were in for a shootout. Forgotten in the noisy chaos was

Wade Duval, a vague outline of deeper black against the diffused darkness of the night.

Stepping back a few paces to gain momentum for his leap, Ki stuck the revolver in his belt and drew the skinning knife, clenching its blade firmly between his teeth. Then he vaulted out into space, and his upreaching arms clamped about Wade Duval in a bear hug. Their two bodies swayed like a pendulum as Ki, with a whispered word in the officer manager's ear, got a tight grip on the rope which was knotted to Duval's wrists. Then, whipping the knife from his teeth with one hand, gripping the rope with the other, Ki slashed the blade savagely against the hempen fibers, six inches above Duval's wrists.

"Over the shaft!" Zugate bellowed from the darkness of a far corner. "I see a knife flashin'. Someone, he is cutting down our hombre!"

Guns stabbed the night with flicking tongues of fire, but Ki's keen blade severed the rope and the two men pitched out of sight into the shaft, a split instant before the salvo of outlaw lead ripped the spot where Duval had been dangling. Straight down into the depths of the mine they hurtled, the elevator cables whistling inches from their heads. The plummeting men landed on Ki's stout rope-and-mesh platform at the level of the crosscut tunnel, and like acrobats striking a circus safety net, they rebounded skyward, to drop on their backs once more on the invisible netting stretched across the shaft well.

Wade Duval tumbled slackly, insensate, dead out again or dead for keeps. Jessie crawled onto the jouncing platform to help Ki move Duval to the crosscut floor. "Thank God, it worked," she said, sighing with relief. "He's alive. I can feel a pulse, a weak but steady heartbeat."

Ki picked up Duval after cutting his wrists and legs free of their bonds, and carried him with Jessie guiding the way through the abysmal black tunnel. Outside, supporting Duval between them, they headed along the slope for the shoulder they had first descended. Midway they dived into a shadowy clump of resinbush and zexmenia, as they saw the bandidos fanning from the shafthouse, gunning for anything they could find.

Wade Duval started coming around just then, semiconsciously twitching and muttering. Ki was about to put a sleeper hold on him when Jessie shook her head and leaned close to Duval, whispering a caution in his ear. He opened his eyes, looked at Jessie unseeingly, and closed them again. But he stayed quiet.

A hollering call from Luiz Zugate fetched his men to the shafthouse steps, where he stood. "We got nothing to worry about, *muchachos*," he told them, his loud voice reaching the trio in the shrubbery. "Whoever shot out the light and tried to rescue Señor Wade, he was *majareta*, crazy in the head. The *asno* fall down the shaft by his own self, saving us the trouble, no?"

Profane laughter, with a nervous ring in it, echoed Zugate's claim.

"Señor Wade drop dead with him, si," Zugate went on, voice rising in complaint. "We never get that safe open now. We daren't blast it open, with the innards full of blasting powders. We cannot make off and hide it to work on; it is too big, too heavy to take fast, or to take far before overgotten. *Que mala suerte*—what bad luck!"

A rumble of comment ensued, in voices pitched too low for Jessie or Ki to catch the words. The prattle ceased as quick as it began, Zugate and crew breaking for their horses. Mounting, they spurred off through the central mine yard, tearing in around the few structures and stockpiles, then headed on down the ore-wagon trail.

One of the bandidos, Ki noticed, rode out of the yard towing a leggy bayard mare by the halter. He glanced at Duval, then at Jessie. "We better get out of here, and pronto. Who knows, they could double back any time."

"Yes, and Wade needs looking over by the doctor."

Once more Duval raised his eyelids. "No doc."

"Nonsense, Mr. Duval. You may have serious internal injuries."

"Wade, Ma'am. The doc left yesterday for Fort Pena."

"No doc. No law," Ki mused thoughtfully. "Have you a bayard mare?" When Duval nodded, Ki said, "No horse, either. They've got it now."

Duval tried to sit up, but Jessie stopped him gently. "We'll help you, Wade. You just take it easy and don't tear yourself up any worse."

Moving on, Jessie and Ki assisted Duval up the slope, across, and down to the pocket hiding their horses. Cinching up, Ki rifled the outlaw's saddlebags and found a spare shirt, tolerably clean, gingham, which he gave Duval to wear. Duval was boosted astride the steeldust grulla, then Jessie swung up behind to support him in the saddle. Duval looked uneasy, as if fearing he'd forget she was a lady—or so it seemed to Ki as he stood alongside, glancing up.

"Aren't you going to mount up?" Jessie queried.

Ki didn't give a direct answer. "Zugate might return anytime, sure. But there might be more of his gang heading this way. Or might not; they might be raiding a ranch instead, might even be the Mashed-O."

"They might be at that," Jessie said. "Yes, I think it probably would be better if you went right to the Mashed-O. I'll catch up with you there as soon as I can."

"Don't worry," Duval told Ki. "My place isn't very far, and we'll take to the brush."

★

Chapter 8

With Wade Duval guiding her horse, and the horse setting its own pace, there wasn't much for Jessie to do but hold on. Which didn't displease her too greatly, and she kept in mind to use a very light and gingerly touch. At times she had to grab him hard, though, causing him acute pain, but less than if he'd fallen off. And more than once she nearly fell off.

It was all Duval's doing. In spite of the pain he brought on himself, he "took to the brush" with a vengeance. There was damn little brush, naturally, but he compensated by leading them through a crazywork of steep arroyos, high-stepped terraces and ravines and buttes and needle crags that would make a mountain goat blanche. Jessie was more than willing to let Duval find their way through. He did, competently, and seemed to be taking the trip well; he was a man of iron, Jessie thought.

Pretty soon they reached a rounded crest. Before her,

Jessie could see a dark valley, with shadowy images of trees and dwellings scattered around the sides.

"We made it," Duval said. "And they're going to be sorry."

Jessie asked, "What do you mean, we made it?"

"I'm home. Well, practically."

"That last little bit can kill you," Jessie said.

Her surefooted grulla picked its way down the slope, and they came to the valley floor obliquely, from the southeast, into a section where most locals seemed to have settled. But only a politico could have claimed the area was a settlement. It was a motley hodgepodge of tents, shanties, adobe cabanas, and *jacale*-style mud hovels that appeared in the darkness like the ground had merely swollen into shack-sized tumors, all dumped helter-skelter among the boulders and interconnected by a tangle of rubbish-strewn footpaths.

Why more folks located here than elsewhere was a mystery to her.

The best she could figure was that misery loves company.

Wade Duval lived in a fringe area, away from the worst, and when they entered his yard, Jessie sighed inwardly with relief. Generally looking in tidy repair, the yard encompassed a typical, single-story, *vigas*-roofed adobe cabana, along with a lean-to stable, corral, and a couple of sheds.

Duval reined in by the front door. Jessie dismounted and helped Duval down from the saddle. All told, the man was in pretty good shape, but weak.

"Good-bye," Duval said. "And thanks again."

"I don't say good-bye until I get you delivered and signed for."

"Whatever you say, ma'am, but ain't nobody here to take me."

Jessie didn't seem to hear. Half-supporting him, she hitched to his tiepost, saying, "I can take care of my horse later," then helped Duval into his house.

Luckily Duval had the old miners' habit of keeping a lamp by the door. After lighting it, Jessie glanced around as she led him inside. There was a bunk across from the window, and a bench by the stove with a bucket and a washbasin. Everything was rough but neat, but lacked doilies and bric-a-brac and other feminine graces. She believed Duval; he wasn't taken by anyone.

Sitting Duval down on his bunk, Jessie went and barred the door and draped the window. Then she sat down on the bunk beside Duval and said, "Well, I guess the first thing is to get that shirt off. Here, I'll help."

Duval reared as if scalded. "The hell you will."

"Don't be silly, Wade. The shirt served its purpose, to keep you warm and your blood off me. But you can't see your injuries, much less treat them, with it on. And the longer it's on, the greater your chance of infection."

"But you—"

"Have seen far worse. Bullet wounds, stabbings, disease, births to deaths. Besides, a girl can't grow up on a ranch without getting an eyeful. So . . ." Very gently she peeled the borrowed shirt off Duval. "Bend forward a bit, Wade. If you can."

Duval leaned over, biting his lip to stifle a groan. Some of the lashings that had drawn blood were bleeding again, his movements having weakened and torn the coagulations. Jessie looked over his gashes, slashes, swollen blotches, and shredded skin. "I don't see any really deep punctures," she said, frowning with concern. "My guess is, with a cleaning and bandaging and maybe an ointment, you just might heal up fine."

Duval tried to make light of it. "Nary a scar, Doc?"

"Probably not, if we treat it promptly. I'm not a doctor, though; I'm just going by how I tend my cows," she said, poker-faced, and stood up. "I'll leave you to take your pants off by yourself. You can wrap the blanket there around you."

"Whoa up! They didn't drop my drawers. Why should you?"

"Not me, you. Your pants are filthy, bloodsoaked. When you hung there, they dropped from your waist to your hips, almost. Your bared lower gut was beaten bloody. How do you clean and heal it, wearing dirty pants waist-high? Moreover, you can't bind yourself. I will."

"Oh."

"Now, what about a bathtub?"

"No tub. We wash up in a stream over the hill."

"Soap?"

There was a pause. Then, nervously: "There're a couple of tonics and nostrums, I thinks, in the cupboard."

"I see. Well, I'll find what I can. Shuck those pants, right now."

A kettle with water in it stood on the stove. There was some kindling stacked beside the stove, and Jessie had no trouble lighting a fire. While the water was heating, she checked the cupboard and other likely spots, careful to avert her eyes as she heard Wade Duval skinning down buff-naked. Unable to look, her imagination conjured an image of Duval naked, causing her taut breasts to tingle, her rosy nipples to harden involuntarily. From their first meeting in the Paydirt, she'd been attracted to the easy grace of his motions, the strong muscles flexing in his chest and legs, the hard bas relief of . . . Whoops! Jessie clenched her buttocks and inner thigh muscles in an attempt to quash the budding tendrils of arousal curling in her belly.

Hastily she poured the now steaming water into a tinned wash basin. "Are you decent, Wade?"

A throat-clearing sounded from across the room.

Presuming that signified he was, Jessie carried the basin to the bunk along with a stool to set it on, some strips of cloth, a bottle of liniment and a jar of iodoform powder. Wade Duval was stretched out on his stomach on the bunk, with the blanket draped decorously around him.

108

When she sat down on the edge of the bunk, he shifted over to give her room, twitchy as a man expecting the mattress to explode. Tickled, she managed not to laugh aloud, but couldn't help smiling bemused as she bathed his wounded back.

He cleared his throat again. "Ain't the hugest bath. Ain't the peak of modesty, either."

"Why, Wade, it's what we make of it."

"True, true . . . or what we don't make of it."

With a tight chuckle, Jessie opened the liniment bottle and sloshed some on his back. Duval flinched, sucked in his breath, his entire body quivering with muscles tensing as though he were fighting a seizure. It proved too much; with a blood-curdling howl, Duval raged, "Greatfuckin' Jehoshaphat! What is that shit? Acid? Or a brandin' iron?"

"Persephassa Gargling Oil Liniment," she answered, quoting from the bottle label. "The Great Internal and External Corrective Reknowned for the Cure of All Malady and Lameness for Ma—"

"Gimme that!" Wrenching around, Duval snatched hold of the bottle, the blanket twisting about his muscular legs as he moved, emphasizing his crotch area. And watching him with admiring eyes, Jessie thought dizzily, *Either Wade's got a shotgun under there, or he's hung like a horse!*

Duval failed to see her reaction or the focus of her attention, suddenly erupting, "For Man or Beast! Says so right here! Why, it's horse rub, for horse wounds!"

"We're all God's creatures," Jessie said, managing to keep a serious expression. "A wound is a wound." She retrieved the bottle. "Lie down."

Skeptically Duval eased flat again, waiting to the liniment to stop burning. Amazingly it did, he reported a moment later, while Jessie continued rubbing tenderly with her fingers . . . and gradually, against her will, she sensed budding tendrils of pleasure beginning to curl deep down in her belly band loins.

"That's all," she said firmly, mainly to herself. "Liniment, I mean. On your back. I'll do your chest, then put on the iodoform and wrap you up."

Duval turned over carefully, a little awkwardly, trying to maintain his modesty and the blanket. He folded his hands and plunked them in his lap, which stretched the blanket that much more over the pocket of his groin. Jessie stared. Her errant ogling caused a slight twinge of self-consciousness to steal through her, and she hastily glanced higher—only to see Duval gazing avidly over her thrusting breasts, seeming to strip them naked.

"Move your arms, and I'll wash your chest," she said amiably, trying hard to retain the last shreds of composure. Then as she set to sluicing his chest with a washrag, she averted her eyes from him, yet could sense his eyes roaming heatedly over the contours of her body. Again self-consciousness stole through her, for she was acutely aware of how she must look to Duval, shabby, dusty, windblown and travel-worn, bleary from a lack of sleep.

Jessie could not see what other people saw, what other men saw. Duval observed her attentively, amd spotted a rent in her clothes, a few scratches on her face and hands, but he ignored them as trivial. It was the smooth tan of her face, the delicacy of her hands that Duval prized; and when she finished washing him and reached for the liniment, it was the way her long hair, tangled and hatless, caught the lampglow and gleamed like the hue of fireweed honey. And as she sat and began rubbing on liniment, Duval viewed all of her as a sensuously beautiful vixen—a tad flowery, and he lacked the gift of gab to say it. Instead he chuckled nervously and placed his hand lightly, affectionately on her leg.

"You're a pretty prime filly to be with, Jessie."

"You're not bad yourself." Jessie touched him softly. Massaging, kneading, her hands eased from where rope wounds started high on one side, down along the ribcage to his lower abdomen just above the start of his loins. Her

110

fingers explored very slowly, erotically, teasing him by working lower along the line of his blanket. She could hear his breath deepening, his pulse quickening, and could feel her own lungs sucking in air, her blood racing with a fire that flamed through her flesh and goaded her to reckless abandon. Her fingers wormed lower, dipping down below the blanket to circle around his hips and thighs.

Trembling, sucking in his breath, Duval started to say something but then paused, his tongue licking his lips as he regarded her. And Jessie could sense it now, the desire stirring within him despite his gentlemanly intentions. He cleared his throat, tried again. "Don't fun me, like I was thinking to take advant—"

"No?" she cut in, a ghost of a smile creasing her mouth. "It never crossed your mind?" She touched his groin once, lightly, and Duval let out a noise like a death rattle. "It's crossing mine, and it's crossing yours, Wade. It certainly looks like you're up to something."

"Guess it shows, eh?" He grinned ruefully, glancing down at his blanket perversely tenting out from his loins, and then gazed smoldering at her, his voice husky. "Well, it 'pears I can't deny that if the lady is willing, I wouldn't dislike a kiss 'tween friends." Then he opened the blanket.

Jessie gave a long, purring sigh as she gazed down at him. "The lady is willing. . . ." Tauntingly, she started undressing, mimicking Duval by first stripping bare from the waist up, revealing firm, succulent breasts with ripe berry nipples springing hard from their tips.

Duval sucked one of the nipples, laving her breast while he fondled her other breast. She wriggled, moaning, almost stumbling while removing her boots and pants, peeling totally naked as his other hand roamed down her curvaceous body. She felt her legs open with a touch of his hands, wanting his hand now, unashamedly standing by the bunk and moving her hips in concert with his fingers sliding up inside her.

Goaded by passion, Duval leaned out from the bunk and

111

planted a kiss on her golden-fleeced loins. Jessie contracted her strong thighs so that the muscular action clamped her moistly welcome passage tightly around his finger. Duval, playing the game, pulled her closer with his hooked fingers, indicating she should join him. Willingly she followed the fingers onto the bunk, and straddled his pelvis with her knees on the bunk on either side of his waist. "I've wanted you since we met, Jessie."

"I know, Wade." Sighing, his fingers igniting her, Jessie obediently slid up straddling Duval's chest almost to his chin, then raised a little on her knees. His fingers quested inside while he leaned up with his face between her splayed creamy thighs. He kissed her deep between her fleshy lips, replacing his fingers with his laving tongue. She felt him thirsting to take her, hungry to possess her. Jessie let her body accept his lust with a fresh feeling of abandon, a frenzy of motion. She spraddled her legs wider and undulated her buttocks up against his greedy ministrations.

She climaxed swiftly, feeling the clenched fist deep up inside her belly, although it was over in brief moments of moaning and fevered bliss. Yet even as her senses were concentrating on chronic spasm, she felt Duval press his mouth closer and reach up with both hands to play with her breasts, his mouth becoming a hungry, hot invader, spearing her with his tongue, nipping tenderly with his lips and teeth. Jessie moaned. A minute . . . two minutes . . . her belly rippled, her hips curved up, her groin grinding against his face with pulsating tension . . .

And Jessie climaxed again. She wailed and twisted in the clutch of her sweet agony, writhing and throbbing . . . but she resisted, managing to break the mouth that played summer lightning against her moist pink flesh. "E-enough," she panted. "You can't take it all, all at once."

Duval grinned. "Well, don't expect me to do more work. I'm hurtin'."

Jessie squirmed back along his waist to straddle his hips, feeling his hot length burning against her crotch. She

112

reached under with her right hand and grasped him, positioning his thick crown between her moist nether lips, her loins absorbing the girth of his spearing shaft as she impaled herself slowly yet eagerly upon it.

She fastened her mouth on his and played moaning, electrifying tongue-games with him. Her stiffened nipples and aching breasts brushed against his chest while she lowered herself, until the last inch of him was driven, throbbing, up inside her belly.

He asked, "Too much? Hurt?"

"Yes . . . *No!*" Jessie wriggled on him and felt his swollen bulk stir and shift in her. She began sliding on him, slowly at first, then with increasing enthusiasm as the erotic sensations intensified. Soon she was pumping deeper, more swiftly, as his shaft surged up into her depths like a fleshy bludgeon, pummeling Duval against the bunk.

His hands grasped her dancing breasts. "Not so hard!"

"Oh, your back, your poor front," she cooed, slowing. "I'm sorry. You just lie there and let me take you nice and easy."

Despite her best intentions, Jessie soon began humping wildly again, bouncing her hips up and down with increasing abandon. She pistoned her tightly gripping loins around his shaft until the bunk squealed in protest, until Duval was no longer aware of his wound and was thrusting in rhythm to her frenzied tempo.

He sucked one swaying breasts into his mouth, flicking her distended nipple with his tongue and grasping her other breast with his hand. Her passion continued building to an insane pitch, feeling his manhood growing ever larger in pending release, seeing his eyes sparkle with lust, and felt his tension and quickening motions. Duval's final, bruising upthrusts triggered her again. She whimpered, sobbing, as her third climax overwhelmed her.

"Ohhh . . . Ohhh . . . !"

She arched and plunged madly, ground herself against him, her passage squeezing, squeezing spasmodically until, bursting, Duval came. She felt him erupt, felt him vibrant and huge within her as he groaned, his body stiffening, his hot juices geysering deep up into her belly.

Then, with the ebb of passion, Jessie crouched limp and satiated over Duval. Slowly, sighing contentedly, she eased off his flaccid body and lay down on the bunk alongside him. Duval wanted to say something, but nothing came out, at a loss for words. Instead, he silently cradled her in his arms and dozed off, their bodies remaining loosely entwined. . . .

Jessie woke up once a short time later. She lay for a moment listening to Duval sleeping comfortably. Then gradually, gently, she sat up and eased from his lax embrace, slipping noiselessly from the bed.

And Duval said, "I'd like you to stay."

"Oh! You startled me. I'd like to stay, too, but . . ."

"Of course, but you've got to leave sometime. I know. Still, I didn't want to lose you. I've a feeling you're a winner."

"Well, I'm not," Jessie said. "But Wade, I'm only going to go take care of my horse."

"Oh." There was another long pause. "You're coming back?"

"Yeah, and I hope to be coming again. . . ."

The second time Jessie awoke, it was still dark. She didn't know the hour and really didn't care. It didn't matter. This time when she eased out of bed, she didn't wake up Duval. And this time she didn't come back.

★

Chapter 9

Dawn had flared, dazzling, in a pink-gold sky by the time Ki reached Mooneye Valley. The mustang was panting harshly, flagging, still game but simply too tuckered to keep up a strong pace. Ki slowed and patted his mount's laboring flanks. There was no sense in killing the animal.

The morning was incandescent, clear, and cloudless, when Ki arrived at the Mashed-O. All was tranquil—in fact, too damn serene for his peace. He saw no one around and, reining in at the ranchouse, heard no sound other than his spraddle-legged horse heaving for breath. Yet there were no signs of struggle or disturbance, which he'd expect to find if something had happened to everybody here.

As he was dismounting, the front door opened and the Mexican housekeeper, Chita, stepped out on the porch. "Just you?" she asked, scanning the yard in dismay. "I hoped Segundo Y'brough, the *vaqueros*, they had returned . . ."

"Chita, what's wrong?"

She moved closer, a stricken expression on her face. "*Es malisimo*—it's terrible! Last night was another attack, cows were stolen, and Señorita Prudence, we fear she was stolen, too.

Ki went rigid. "Y'mean outlaws broke in here, made off with her?"

"The Señorita was out, out herding. She insisted the rancho was hers, her duty, and it was up to her to hold it or lose it. A muy fina lady, señor, but oh so *fantoche*."

Meaning pigheaded, in border slang. Pru could be that, Ki agreed; she had grit, the kind of spit-in-the-eye tenacity that could bring her through alive. It led him to ask, "Anyone else missing or got hurt?"

"Not missing, señor, and not many hurt, at least not badly. All but three rode out at daybreak, in such a fury to catch the *villanos* that they left the three"—Chica glanced at the stable, crossing herself—"for their return."

"It's dicey to wait in this heat," Ki said. Offering to take care of the *problemo*, he walked his mount across to the stable. Near inside he found the bullet-torn bodies of three nighthawks, recognizing them from the earlier raid. They lay open to the flies, their odors of violence and human death boogering the horses in the closeby stalls, though having no effect on the jaded mustang.

After covering the bodies with old horseblankets, Ki tended to the mustang and turned it into the corral. His hammerhead roan was in there, too, rested and rasty, revived from its exhausted condition of the morning before last, following the raid and chase. He'd had to ride to Quevidas, then, on a mount from the ranch cavvy; it'd been that horse he'd left at Chaldeen's Gridiron spread, but saddled with the gear Ki had transferred from the hammerhead.

He buried the nighthawks at the end of the barn, where the soil was looser and easier to spade up. There was a custom, not generally much discussed but often practiced, of dividing the effects of the deceased amount the survivors concerned. Ki avoided the custom like poison. Guns, wallets, clothes, boots, everything was scrupulously collected and so interred, for if there were repercussions later for any cause, he'd be able to say, "Here they are, exactly as I put them away. Untouched. Nothing missing."

While he had the opportunity, however, Ki searched the bunkhouse and environs and through everybody else's belongings as well. Nothing was kept; all and sundry were meticuously returned as found, for much the same reasons.

This took time, of course. It was approaching noon when Ki finished the burials, cloudy with rage, and cleaned the dirt from the spadeblade with a corncob like any good gardener. Then he went and brought his hammerhead out in front of the stable, and began to saddle up using gear from the mustang.

Jessie had not as yet shown up. Ki was tempted to backtrack to the mine, just in case. Or he could chase after the Mashed-O crew, though he doubted he'd overtake them, surely not in time to be much use, if any. And mindful of where and how he'd been kept, of course, he felt that Chaldeen and his Gridiron deserved a return visit. But he couldn't waste time sticking around here; he had to go do something, even if it was wrong.

Happening to look up from tightening the saddle cinch, he glimpsed the outline of a rider coming a long way off. He shaded his eyes, pulling his hat-brim lower, trying to discern the heat-hazy figure, and realized it was a woman. There was something in her motion. Too supple at the waist, her shoulders too limber, body blending with rhythmic sway of her horse.

As she drew nearer, Ki laughed at himself and stepped out into view. Yes, it was a woman. It was Jessie. She waved, spurring forward to meet him, and reined in alongside with her hair tousled and looking sleepily disheveled, as if just out of bed. Wisely Ki did not ask. No need,

117

really; the sparkle in her eyes and her contented canary smile were naked giveaways.

Jessie glanced at Ki and chilled, losing her smile. Despite his try at a welcoming grin, his face was hardened with stone-cold savagery. "Ki, what is it?" she gasped, dismounting. "What's happened?"

"Plenty." Brief and to the point, Ki related the news as Jessie listened in angry alarm. "Since there was nothing to gain by waiting for the crew," he concluded, "I was getting ready to head for the Gridiron outfit."

"You think they're holding Prudence?"

"There's a chance. If not her, they're holding answers."

"Can't pass that up. Let me saddle another horse and we'll go."

"Now, Jessie," Ki began, "you're just in from a long ride, and—"

"Don't 'Now, Jessie' me. I'm in no worse shape than you after that ride, and I bet you haven't gotten any more rest than I have, either."

"Well, I dozed asaddle much of the way."

"So did I. It's answers I need, not sleep. Or waiting. Even if Zugate and Murillo were hunted down, there's still El Cascabel to deal with."

"Señorita Jessie! Señor!" Chita was calling from the porch, gesturing with a ladle. "Put your horses away and come eat. You must be hungry, si?"

"*Me estoy muriendo de hambre*—I'm starving," Jessie replied, smiling. "But we're about to leave, Chita. Can you pack some food for us to take?"

Chita nodded, and went back in.

"Assuming Brazos Chaldeen is there with the answers," Jessie said as they started for the stable, "why would he give them to us, or anything else except a hard time?"

Ki shrugged. "I've a feeling that Chaldeen is being pressured. If so, maybe we can discover what's forcing him to knuckle under, then maybe add a little or take some off."

"And maybe that's how Chaldeen will answer us—adding a little soft soap and shaving off some truth. Say he's El Cascabel, just for the arguement, Ki. If he could pin suspicions on someone else, he'd feel a great deal easier."

Ki smiled tight, his mouth crimping at the corners. "Yeah, I imagine most any man would lie like a grass fire to a avoid a hangnoose."

In short order Jessie's weary grulla was tended and corralled, and her saddle gear was slapped on a fresh Mashed-O horse. Chita appeared, armloaded with provisions. "Leftovers from breakfast," she insisted, and fussed when they couldn't all cram into the saddlebags. Thanking her, they heeled their horses into a stretching lope out through the ranchyard entrance. They didn't look back, but they could feel Chita's imploring eyes following them.

Through Mooncye Valley they headed for the Rio Grande, then paralleled it south by southwest, riding expeditiously yet cautiously along the flanks of Boquillas Canyon. Ravine emptied into ravine, and the straited walls were honeycombed with caves and crevices and side canyons, crooked and unexplored, every one of them a spot for ambush.

Heat lay like a suffocating weight, the sun scorching their bent backs. After a few miles Ki reined in to study the deceiving perspectives. Moving on, he led Jessie on a more westerly course, gradually angling away from the river toward a distant line of low mottled hills, fuzzy in the sunglare.

Approaching, Ki carefully scanned the rimline of the hills. "I think this is the range. If so, Gridiron's on the other side. I left there eastbound, then looped north along the far slopes, and rode westward to the wagon road."

When they reached the hills, they climbed up and over the crest by whatever path or terrain appeared easiest. Descending along the western slopes, they reached a high vantage point where Jessie caught her first glimpse of the chapel. The Gridiron ranchstead was not yet visible in the hollow below the chapel. They moved on down in a broad sweep that brought them around behind the chapel from almost due east, along a drywash below the rear bank of the rise.

The remaining distance was open ground, with the bank deep in gravel and loose shale. Their mounts couldn't help but make noise plowing uphill. So ground-reining the horses, they took their saddle carbines and continued afoot, climbing lightly, carefully, to the flat top of the rise, then angling toward the blind backside of the chapel. The rise appeared deserted, the squalid huts empty. They glided forward along the wall of the chapel until they could view beyond the rise, down into the Gridiron ranchstead.

Horses stood banded before the main cabin.

Crouching, Ki murmered, "Looks like Chaldeen has guests."

"Or that Prudence has guards," Jessie whispered pointedly.

"Well, let's take a gander inside the chapel first. Leastwise see up around front here, if the door is bolted or not."

They advanced stealthily, almost crawling by the time they reached the corner of the chapel. Motioning for Jessie to stay back, Ki sprang out a step to glance at the front door—

And collided with a man thrusting around the corner.

Sombreroed, hulking, a revolver in hand, the man was a bandido who had apparently been stationed as a lookout up in front of the chapel. Whatever had drawn him to the corner, he was startled by the impact, though he rebounded instantly, firing twice. The second shot was pure reflex; he was already dead. Both shots sailed off harmlessly into the sky as he went over backward with the hilt of a skinning knife protruding from the loose flesh beneath his chin. Ki had been just a bit faster, bringing the point of the knife upward with savage force, plunging it through muscle and tendon into the brain stem.

As the bandido hit the ground on his back, there came from inside the cabin a confusion of shoutings and stompings. Jessie now fired, striking the first man who showed in the cabin doorway. He slumped, but could not fall for the crush of others behind him, frenzied by the gunfire. Jessie triggered again. Howling, jerking the man in and slamming the door, they poked gunbarrels through the windows and began unleashing a torrent of lead at the rise.

Bellying flat, Jessie and Ki measured their remaining shots, forcing the gunmen to hunker in the cabin, stalling a counterattack. They might be able to outrun that bunch back to their horses, but they couldn't outrun bullets down the open rear bank of the rise. Yet once the bandidos recovered their wits and realized there were only two up by the chapel, they'd come after them . . . and if they didn't get them on the run, they'd spread out hunting them on horseback.

In a desperate gamble Ki began working backward, whispering to Jessie, "Keep them pinned." Once out of sight of the cabin, he rose and raced around the back of the chapel and came up the other side, again making sure he wasn't seen by those below. Then, with a few well-placed shots to draw their attention, Ki shouted at the top of his lungs: "In the name of the State of Texas, y'all are under arrest! Surrender! Y'all are surrounded, boys, and it's death if you fight!"

He got a reaction, though not quite what he expected. The bandidos broke, leaping out the door and windows, swinging into saddle with pistols bucking, lead covering their panicked retreat. From the rise he and Jessie sent crashing volleys with deadly precision, dropping another man and wounding a couple more who managed to hang on, routing the survivors as they spurred south toward the haven of Mexico.

Picking herself up off the ground, Jessie brushed the dust off her clothes. She glanced swiftly at Ki, her face showing concern when she saw blood on his arm.

"A scratch," Ki assured her. "That was a hot reception."

"Too hot. We must've stepped into something important."

Hoping that the something involved Prudence, they swiftly checked the chapel. It was empty. Then they headed down to the cabin, carbines held ready. The bandido who had fallen in the yard was dead; another corpse could be seen lying inside the threshold of the front door. But as they drew closer to the cabin, Ki called out a warning to Jessie and halted suddenly. He had heard a low moan and then a faint sound of a body dragging over dirt. Three long strides brought him to the door. He jumped inside, flattening himself against the wall, carbine leveled.

A man stretched full length on the floor, his face grimacing in pain. Blood formed a deep stain along his right side and his pinched face was pale and gleaming with sweat. Jessie came sprinting through the doorway and crouched, ready for trouble, and stared at the wounded man.

"This guy isn't a bandido," Jessie said. "He's . . . Isn't he Mad?"

"Uh-huh. Madison Knecht, Chaldeen's right-hand pard."

Jessie stepped over to Mad Knecht. He looked at her as though through a haze that half-blinded him, and attempted to drag himself away. Stopping him, Jessie ripped open the bloody shirt and examined the bullet hole, while Ki made a quick search of the cabin and outlying structures. He did not find Prudence or anyone else. Somewhat surprisingly, in the corral was the Mashed-O horse he'd been riding when taken prisoner, and hanging in the cabin was his vest, undisturbed, as though Chaldeen had anticipated his return.

Mad Knecht's wound needed doctoring. The slug had penetrated low on the right side, ranging toward the backbone, and had either smashed a vertebrae or was lodged against one, for his legs were paralyzed. Jessie cast Ki a significant look when he came back, and Mad Knecht seemed to catch it.

"Is it bad?" Mad Knecht wheezed.

"Not if we reach a doctor," Jessie said. "I think we might be able to straighten you up when we get you back to the Mashed-O."

"Patch me up, so I can dance at the end of a hangnoose later on? Thanks, but I'd druther cash."

"Maybe you won't, Mad. You can talk your way out of a noose."

"About Brazos? Nope. I ain't got a thing to say."

Jessie didn't press the matter. Ki went after the horses as she cleaned Mad Knecht's wound and fashioned a crude bandage. The ride would be painful, but she believed that Mad Knecht would reach the Mashed-O and get medical help in due course. Together she and Ki raised Mad Knecht to the saddle and tied him there securely by means of a belt hooked over the saddle horn. They started back, riding slowly, their pace adjusted to what Mad Knecht could withstand. Shortly he grew feverish, and before long lapsed unconscious, mumbling incoherently. Other than keeping his face mopped and his mouth wetted, there was little they could do for him.

It was going on early evening when they arrived at the ranch. The crew was back, milling about the yard, and they needed but one look at the dejected faces to guess the rustlers had eluded capture. Prudence was still a prisoner.

Vaughn Yarbrough met them, grim-visaged, with whiskey on his breath. He did not seem surprised when Jessie recounted the gunplay at the Gridiron, but his muddy eyes widened when she told him of the wounded Mad Knecht and asked that a hand be sent for the doctor. Yarbrough's lips twisted in anger.

"His sort don't deserve no sawbones, Miz Jessie."

"I don't treat any man that way."

"They never gave us no chance. T'was just before dawn, still dark, and Miz Pru was standin' her share guard, when them varmints shot the nighthawks and ran off with her and the herd. By time we rallied, they was out of sight and hearin'. We followed, but lost their tracks down by the Devil's Backbone and scoured for miles 'round without picking up any sign of 'em. Well, they ain't going to get away with it, none of 'em. Let this 'un die.''

"Mexican bandidos led by Luiz Zugate pulled the raid," Jessie countered. "Zugate takes his orders from a cantina owner named Felipe Murillo."

"In Quevidas!" Yarbrough snapped. "Why, we'll wipe that rathole off the map. I'll string them two muckers personally to the nearest cottonwood limb."

Jessie shook her head. "Not right away. There're too many outlaw guns in Quevidas, and the Mashed-O crew wouldn't last long enough to cross the Rio. Besides, there's a third man backing Felippe Murillo's play, at least most of it. He's the fellow we really need to get."

Yarbrough clenched his fists. "Who is he?"

"We only know for sure that he's Anglo. Ki overheard him."

"Heard him? Did you see him, Ki? Wouldn't you know him?"

"Afraid not," Ki admitted, and gave a brief version of following Zugate to the meeting at the shack, his subsequent capture and escape.

Yarbrough frowned thoughtfully. "Ask me, ain't no question. You was held at the Gridiron, had a run-in with bandidos there, and Brazos Chaldeen appears to've hit the trail. He's your gringo."

"Maybe. Maybe not. We'll find out as soon as Mad Knecht tells us," Jessie said impatiently. "Have someone fetch the doctor, and if the doctor's not back in town yet, have him wait. I want this man to talk, don't you?"

Opening his mouth to object, Yarbrough seemed to realize he was on the losing end of the arguement, and grudgingly gave the necessary orders. Soon a ranchhand rode away for the doctor. "Waste of good hoss sweat," Yarbrough growled, stumping off to the bunkhouse. "I'll make sure Mad Knecht sings before he croaks."

Mad Knecht was made comfortable in one of the guest rooms. By nightfall he seemed to be better, his fever down and his ramblings less demented. Jessie and Ki sat in the room with him. Out in the patio they could see the glow of Vaughn Yarbrough's cigarette.

Suddenly Ki straightened, listening. Jessie also caught the sound.

"Horses. But it's far too soon for the doctor."

As they went outside, three riders hailed the ranch and then loomed up in the lamplight: Big Nick Tualatin, the smily Leo Frost, and Wade Duval, still suffering the effects of his torture. Vaughn Yarbrough appeared and blurted the news about the raid and Prudence Oliver's abduction.

"Then why're you hanging around here?" Big Nick Tualatin demanded, scowling. "Why ain't you out after 'em?"

"We was, all day we was. But they know the country like we don't, and they just faded away. Up rock walls, into blank stone—somewheres."

Frost shook his head. "Miz Starbuck, Ki, we came to thank you for saving Wade's skin and our own, the payroll. Sad to 'fess it took suchlike to wake us up, but now this! This's too much. Men don't steal ladies in Texas."

"Sounds like she was in no place fit for a lady," Duval asserted, glaring at Yarbrough. "How could you permit it?"

"I couldn't prevent it," Yarbrough argued crossly. "Miz Pru's the owner. And any gent so foolish as to stop her from doin' her want had best chain her to something solid." He jerked his thumb at Jessie. "How'soever, Miz Starbuck and Ki brung us a prisoner from the Gridiron. They think he'll maybe talk after the sawbones revivifies him."

Nodding, Tualatin had a word with Leo Frost, then declared, "You just learned us that to save ourselves we got to fight together, so you ain't fighting this alone. Wade, you stay with Leo and help get after Miz Oliver. I figure I got the clout to spread the word, to go recruit the miners. Won't be hard agin' gal rustlers. The most warty-faced, rum-addled pitman knows wimmen is sacred scarce. She can be ugly enough to burst a muley bull's gall bladder, and even then she has to be protected, just for the sake of the breed if for nothing more.''

Shortly after Big Nick Tualatin had started his long ride back to Ingot, Chita announced a snack was in order and assaulted the kitchen with a frenzy. As they all began heading for the dining room, Ki remarked to Duval, ''You're walking slightly game-leg, Wade. Hurt bad?''

''I got nothing wrong,'' Duval replied. ''Just a little stiff.''

''Oh, more than a little stiff,'' Jessie murmered, deadpan.

Duval reddened from the neck up.

At the table, palaver centered on ending the outlaws without ending Miss Pru, a frustrating dilemma. Ki went to check on Knecht, leaving Jessie to field questions from Leo Frost and veiled hints by Yarbrough that she should confide in him. Mainly, though, the quandary seemed to whet their appetites, and with Wade Duval, they almost managed to lay waste to Chita's mountainous platters and bottomless coffeepot.

Chita was removing the dishes to the kitchen when Ki appeared in the doorway. ''Jessie,'' he said. ''Mad Knecht wants to talk to you.''

Jessie roused from her chair and hurried out. Frost, Duval, and Vaughn Yarbrough trooped after, halting at the threshold of the guest room. Mad Knecht's eyes burned feverish, yet he appeared aware of Jessie and gratified to see her.

''Tell me gospel,'' he wheezed. ''Is Starbuck here hunting Brazos?''

''I don't know anyone after Chaldeen or if he's even wanted. Not by me.''

''So Ki told me. He'd told Brazos that, too, Brazos told

me. But I had to hear it from you." Abruptly a fit of coughing rendered Knecht exhausted.

Compassionately Jessie said, "Rest, now. I'll be by later."

Knecht made a slight negative gesture with his hands. "I'm due to cash in, I feels it. Time to rest then," he panted. "Talking at all runs against my grain. And I ain't talking to you 'cause I'm liking you, you and your kind. But somebody ought to know, so it won't die with me. Somebody who won't use it against Brazos. I'm talking to you 'cause I'm trusting you, forced to."

Knecht began laboring for breath. "Relax, don't strain," Jessie advised, sitting down beside the bed. Ki moved next to her, and the three men in the doorway shifted restlessly. Jessie spoke in a low, warm voice both encouraging and centering on a start. "Go on, Mad, when you can. What were those bandidos doing at your ranch today?"

"They came to fetch the Gridiron over to their hideout south of Quevidas. Brazos was to rebrand a herd there and us crew was to drive 'em back across the Rio to a shipping point north of here."

"On whose say-so?"

"Murillo, and Zugate. Too big for their boots, and sneakier than suck egg weasels. But Brazos, he ain't one with 'em, honest."

"Then why's Chaldeen mixed up in their rustling?"

"Same reason I am. We had some law trouble years back, shortly after our last tangle with your Circle Star. A cow heist gone bad. Winged a sheriff. Me an' Brazos, we escaped, but the law jailed and killed the rest of our gang. Taught us a lesson—" Knecht choked and stiffened, a spasm of pain knotting his face.

"Easy," Jessie soothed, "take it easy."

Knecht nodded. "W-We tried to go straight. Took up a small ranch near Abilene, but Brazos ain't unheard of. In due time the word got out. We got out before the law got wind. Came down here t-to the Big Bend to try again. . . ."

He began muttering, breathing raggedly. "An' we was getting by, till he . . . till . . ."

"Till who?" Jessie pressed, seeing the fast-surging flush of fever.

"Brazos, me, knew all about us . . . Do as told, or face forever an' amen in calaboose . . . Keep eye on them, too big for their boots. He can't let us free now, his ace in the hole . . . Tired of runnin'. Hogtied . . ."

"Who, Mad?" Jessie insisted. "Tell me, who's the man?"

Struggling against delirium, Knecht opened his lips to answer, hesitated. Jessie crouched forward, Ki leaned closer, and the three in the doorway were peering breathless. His lips started to move . . . then Knecht lapsed incoherent again, rambling aimlessly and wildly. Jessie's face fell and Ki swore under his breath.

The men in the doorway stirred, and Jessie looked around at them. Wade Duval looked amazed as he stared at the writhing figure on the bed. Leo Frost seemed thoughtful and puzzled. Vaughn Yarbrough's muddy eyes fastened on Mad Knecht's ruddy face as though he were trying to tear the man's secret from the babbling tongue.

Leaving the room with Ki, Jessie closed the door firmly in the faces of the other three men. "Cold compresses, gentlemen," she asserted, "are about the only help for him now. I'll ask Chita to make some up."

"Rotten luck, what rotten luck," Duval groused, discouraged.

Ki shook his head. "Good luck, first catching him, then his talking."

"Now his raving," Frost argued, "and next him dying."

"Knecht won't be dying, not yet. He probably will without a doctor, of gangrene or some other infection, or perhaps the fevers. This one will run its course," Jessie explained, "and as soon as he's lucid again, we'll learn the key man to all this Big Bend trouble."

"That bein' the case," Yarbrough said, "I reckon one

of us had better be with that jasper all the time in case he gets ready. I'll stand watch for a couple of hours.''

"Fine," Jessie agreed. "We can give the compresses while we're at it. Ki, would you relieve Vaughn. I'll take over after I get some rest. Vaughn, have the crew ready to ride in the morning, loaded for bear. When we have the rest of his facts, we'll pick up the cattle trail at the Devil's Backbone or wherever, and come to a showdown with Zugate, Murillo, and their border scum.''

The group broke up. Yarbrough went first to the bunkhouse to pass orders to the men, then returned to the guest room to keep vigil over their valuable prisoner. It seemed a long time before the Mashed-O settled down to quiet. Hands moved around outside, smoking and jawing and prepping weapons and gear for the morning ride. Jessie could hear Ki stirring around his room. She lay in the darkness staring up at the ceiling she could barely see.

It was about over. Come morning they'd know the identity of El Cascabel and the mask that protected him would be shed. Jessie relished the thought. Yet somehow she had a nagging sense, an uncomfortable impression, that something was amiss. It was as though there were too many angles and blind trails to this murderous puzzle to be wrapped up quite so simply and easily.

Far away, a coyote howled. Its mate answered. More distant still was the gruntlings of javelinas, sounds multiplied by echoes from a hundred pinnacles and cliffs. A bird warbled in the chaparral; insects set up a shrill chirping chorus.

A pistol shot split the night with startling suddenness.

Jessie heard a muffled shout and then the pistol blasted again. She jumped to the door, jerked it open. Light streamed from Mad Knecht's room and Vaughn Yarbrough could be heard cursing violently. There was another shot, from within the room. Dashing inside, she saw Yarbrough at the open window, leveling his revolver out into the darkness. He rocked back again. Jessie joined him just in time to glimpse a shadowy figure dodge around the corral and disappear.

"Got clean fuc—er, far away, the knife-tossin' renegade! Look at Mad Knecht, Miz Jessie."

Jessie turned and stared at the bunk. The haft of a heavy knife projected from Knecht's chest. A single glance at the blank staring eyes told Jessie that Knecht would never talk again. This path to El Cascabel had been lost.

Plunging into the room, Ki saw Knecht and his face clouded and his lips clamped in anger. He gave Jessie a smoldering glance and sank in a chair. Leo Frost appeared in the doorway, and a moment later Wade Duval's curious face peered over his shoulder.

"There goes the luck we was talking about," Duval said, glumly.

Yarbrough told what had happened, and answered questions. He knew little. "I thought I heard a noise in the hall, and I stepped to the door to find out about it. Then, while my back was turned, it happened. A knife flashed in through the winder. There's a movement outside, so I throws down at it quick. I missed and he ducked away. I had another chance or two, but it was sure tricky shootin'. He got plumb away."

"Did you have a glimpse of his face?" Frost asked.

"Nope. Happened too quick and the jasper had his hat-brim pulled down over his eyes."

Jessie sighed. "Let's go around the room. Wade, where were you?"

Duval grinned nervously. "In my room. I hadn't undressed yet."

"Mr. Frost, how about you?"

The smily face registered surprise. "Me? I was settin' on my cot trying to figure this hash out. It's got me more discombobulated than a rat-tailed horse at fly time."

Jessie passed her hand, in a tired gesture, over her face. "I know how you feel. Vaughn, will you check your crew? I don't think any are guilty, but we better do it and avoid having to say we overlooked it. Find out if any of them were out of the bunkhouse about the time of the killing.''

Vaughn Yarbrough left the room and Jessie stared thoughtfully at the corpse on the bunk. So. Wade Duval and Leo Frost were alone in their rooms. Either one could have left, thrown the knife, and then ducked around the corner and back to the room. Yarbrough himself might have used his knife, but that left the prowler unaccounted for. The unknown might have been from the Gridiron, trying to learn what had happened to Mad Knecht, or . . . Jessie glanced up as Yarbrough returned.

''Every man-jack wears a clean brand out there,'' Yarbrough reported. ''Not one of 'em left the bunkhouse until the shooting went off.'' His face was dark in stiff, clotted rage and, Jessie suspected, a snort or two of whiskey. ''Well, these stinkin' owlhoots have done a good day's work. They got away with the herd and Miss Pru, and killed three good men—all right four.''

''They haven't got away with anything yet,'' Jessie replied. ''According to Knecht, the herd is hidden out south of Quevidas for brand-blotting, and then is to be driven north. Must be a regular cattle trail worn to that hideout by now. Odds are the herd's there. But if it's gone, it's traveling slow, still blowed from the stampede and border crossings. We can catch up with them if we look sharp.''

Ki spoke up: ''There's also Quevidas. Felipe Murillo's cantina must be used as a sort of clearing station for wet beefs. I figure it's there Zugate and the bandidos make connection with buyers for the next herd, or whatever. When we corner Murillo and Zugate, we'll have Miss Pru safe again.''

''Glory, it's worth trying!'' Frost declared. ''What's the first move?''

''Turning in for the night,'' Ki replied, rising. ''We

can't take Quevidas ram-on. It's going to take some out-smartin', and we may as well sleep on it.''

Yarbrough nodded. "I'm sure hankerin' to get some of them bandidos in my gunsights.''

"I've a mighty strong hunch that you will," Ki promised. "G'night.''

When only he and Jessie remained in the room, they took a last look around, closed the door, and started along the corridor to their rooms. Jessie, mulling, turned and looked sternly at Ki.

"Well?''

"Well, what?''

"Well, what's your surefire idea for outsmartin' Quevidas?''

"I haven't any, none at all.'' Smiling blandly, he went in his room.

For Jessie, sleep proved elusive.

★

Chapter 10

As soon as dawn had lightened enough to see by, the Mashed-O once more saddled up and rode out after the kidnapping rustlers. They retraced the trail of their widelooped herd to the foot of the Dead Horse Peaks, then across into the Devil's Backbone, a forbidding stone chaos of angles, planes, strata and cleavages. The signs grew fainter, fewer, and farther between. The crew had not forgotten, though, the trail they had painstakingly unraveled through the maze of connecting gulches and arroyos and ridge-flanking benches.

Presently the tracks petered out to nothing.

Yarbrough called a halt, as he had the day before, but there wasn't time today to send the crew out searching for signs. Losing the trail had really stung their chief tracker, a seamy-faced ol' cowhand named Sweetwater; he also was second under Yarbrough—would've made foreman if Yarbrough hadn't moved in—and took it out on the crew,

133

as tetchy as a sore-headed dog. Sweetwater was hardest on himself, however, when he came over to see Ki.

"Two hundred in that herd, and I couldn't find nary a cowpat beyond here," he deplored. "I must've missed something, somewhere, damned if I savvy how."

Ki nodded noncommittally. He didn't care about the trail; he'd come here to see where this lined up with the Rio, and the lay of the land in between. They were on the pointy end of a spearhead-shaped plateau, sterile of growth, wedged like a rock delta at the juncture of foothill slopes. From here, the delta continued to widen at a good ten-degree fan into the distance. Nothing ahead or on either side appeared to be menacing enough or attractive enough to head for, and there was nothing between but blank stone.

The possibilities of direction were many. The probabilities of detection were shit.

"A good Apache in a war party," Ki said conversationally, "can tell from horse-sign males from females, by how they let down their droppings and make their water on mesquite. That bests most of us. But their best can't read sign where there is none."

"You saying I didn't miss anything, after all?"

"Can't swear to it, I haven't looked. Offhand, I could believe it. Maybe that's what you missed, Sweetwater, the confidence in yourself."

Ki said no more. By Sweetwater's face, he'd said plenty.

Leaving the plateau, the riders headed for the Rio Grande. They hit the river north of the Devil's Backbone and the Boquillas Canyon stretch, and began following its banks southward, looking for tracks. They also began following Ki's advice, spreading out in case the outlaws should have placed lookouts or had planned an ambush.

No challenge came. They turned up plenty of tracks, not surprisingly. Deer tracks, wolf and rabbit tracks, snake tracks, lizard tracks, bird tracks, wet cow and wild steer tracks, horse tracks, even snail tracks. And among the muddle of prints, somewhere along the miles of popular stomping grounds, were tracks of Mashed-O livestock crossing the Rio.

Nobody could tell just exactly where the midnight run had forded. They knew the herd had gone from trail's end on the plateau, and had come to wind up just south of Quevidas. It also stood to reason that the rustlers, having shaken pursuit, would've driven the herd straightaway for the river—or as straight as the lay of the land would allow—and wouldn't have dawdled getting out of there, either. So they concentrated their search accordingly, within these boundary points.

Ki was riding ahead with Jessie and some others, when they hit a low scooped portion of the bank, and found a swath of deep-punched hoofprints of horses and cattle filled with water. Ki swung down and hunkered on his heels, studying them. Rio Grande water carried a yellowish silt that separated slowly, but this had cleared enough to show the prints were over a day old. The crisp, well-defined projections of the prints indicated they weren't more than a couple of days old, three tops.

Everybody grouped around, heartened, impatient.

"We're on to 'em now," a waddie exulted, "and t'hell with the border!"

Leo Frost laughed. "Say, I believe you really mean it."

The crew chorused their resolve. "The border don't seem to mean much to them crooks, either," another hand roared.

"It's open season on gringo ranchers both sides of the line," Yarbrough growled, "and I got no authority except what I carry on my hip. But b'gawd, I'm raking rowels and crossing south o' the river."

They all raked rowels and crossed south of the river, picking up the cattle tracks. On the wet ground the trail was easy to follow. Not so easy, however, when it veered more to the west and entered the mountainous terrain that flanked the Rio Grande. Here the soil was stony and hard,

135

akin to the plateau. But Ki's keen notice caught broken twigs, bent grass blades, and overturned stones the others would have passed unnoticed.

A few miles farther on, the trail cut sharply down a sag, then south out over a rumpled valley plain toward a distant line of hills. Yonder to their left, sunlight glinted off the huddled squalor of Quevidas. They negotiated the slope with little difficulty, the Mashed-O chafing to spur on toward the hills, but when they reached the valley floor, Ki turned his horse eastward.

"Where're *you* going?" Jessie demanded.

"Quevidas," Ki replied. "Zugate and Murillo may be there, and we don't want them to escape."

Nodding, Jessie shifted to follow. Yarbrough also turned east, and the rest of the Mashed-O hands moved to join suit.

But Ki shook his head. "Like I said last night, Quivedas is going to take some outsmartin', and too big a crowd is liable to smear the deal."

"You figure to go it alone?" Yarbrough snorted.

"Would sort of help to have two or three dependable gents along with Jessie," Ki admitted. "Maybe Duval and Leo Frost, since they're not crew."

"That's sense," Frost said, agreeing.

"One more man will be enough," Ki said. "You come along, Vaughn."

Yarbrough smiled. "Be my pleasure. Sweetwater? Can you handle the trailing with the boys?"

"Them's my boss an' her beefs that's been stole," Sweetwater declared, "And I aim to bring 'em back so long as I'm able to fork the hull."

Ki said, "Fine, trail them to the foot of the hills and wait for us."

"Just to the hills," Sweetwater agreed, though he looked disappointed, "but I'd sure like to keep travelin'."

"Too dangerous," Ki said. "For us, not only you. We could come right behind you or be gone an hour or so, and be hightailin' from some angry gunners when we show. We've got to be able to find you fast, where you can cover us. In any event, Sweetwater, you can bet on action a-plenty when we get back.''

After the two groups parted company, heading their separate ways, Jessie rode beside Ki and wondered just what the devil he was up to.

She knew he was up to something, him and his outsmartin' routine. Long ago she'd learned that when Ki sported an air of innocence as thick as molassas, it usually was to camouflage some hellacious scheme. Moreover, he had armed himself from the stock of weaponry kept at the ranch. At his waist, worn rather high after the style of men who spend much time in the saddle, was a .44-40 Colt Frontier.

He carried a second .44-40 as a spare in a latched-down saddle holster, and a Winchester .44-40 carbine had replaced the off-caliber Express in his saddle scabbard. By his bulging pockets, she reckoned he was packing enough ammunition to sink a gunboat.

Jessie had been wondering, of course, since early that morning. She hadn't asked, knowing Ki wouldn't tell her until he felt ready, and suspecting she didn't want to hear what he would say. How right she was, Jessie discovered before they reached Quevidas, when Ki called a halt ''for a powwow.'' After listening to his plan, she just about turned the powwow into a wardance, but her protests did little good.

Ki went ahead with things his way. . . .

Alone, Ki rode into Quevidas as dark, swarthy heads drew hastily back from glassless windows. Curses followed him in soft whispers down the straggling street to the plaza and ended in Felipe Murillo's cantina. And it was a villainous crew inside the cantina when he entered, looking as though they would rather cut a throat without pay than to find a pile of silver under their chairs. Six men at a greasy card table in the corner did not even glance up from under their sombreros, the same big, sloppy-brimmed kind that he had seen on Zugate and many of the bandidos.

Felipe Murillo leaned on the long bar, staring at Ki, his face inscrutable. *"Buenas dias,"* he grunted as Ki approached. *"Tengo mucho gusto de encontrarle."*

"That's nice," Ki nodded. "I'm glad somebody is pleased to meet me. There's a young lady missing, Señorita Oliver, owner of the Mashed-O. Your friends here might stir out to find her and bring her back safely."

"A missing señorita?" Murillo's eyes widened with mock surprise. "But how could that be?"

"She was kidnapped." Ki looked the bartender squarely in the eyes. "I've an idea you know all about it—and did from the start. You're Felipe Murillo, and Luiz Zugate doesn't steal a corncob to wipe his ass without squaring it with you."

"Señor, you cannot talk to me as if I'm a dog!" Murillo suddenly started to straighten. "I am a gentleman—"

"You're a liar—a damned, cheap cutthroat of a liar!" Ki cut in.

A pistol shot in that quiet room would not have been much louder than the sudden smack of Ki's big hand across the bar. It caught Murillo on the side of the face, hurled him to one side, threw him off his feet, and sent him smashing down on the glassware on the drainboard under the bar.

Ki half-whirled now, his eyes watching everything. He saw the shock that had gone over the crowd. It was as if something had jarred the cantina with a blow. The men at the card table tensed, two of them flinching as if about to get to their feet. That was all that did happen. There was just that one shock, that tenseness, those flinching jerks, and the room was still.

"Señor . . . ." Murillo was stumbling to his feet, a thin line of blood seeping from the left corner of his mouth. "You—"

"I didn't come here to argue. You and Zugate swiped

Señorita Oliver along with her cattle. You know it. I know it. Get some of your scummy lice to fetch her here, pronto.''

"I never took this female. I never seen her. You're loco!''

"Don't start to yap back at me!'' Ki's hand lifted again warningly. "I'll knock you into hellangone. You know what you've got to do. And now I'm walking out the door. Get this: If a shot is fired or a knife thrown, I'll wheel and pump this room full of lead—and the first man I'll kill will be Felipe Murillo, and that's you, you pinched-beak jackel.''

"Si, señor.'' There was murder shining in Murillo's eyes now. They were hot little eyes, as quick as triggers in their glancing about. "But let us suppose that nobody goes to look for the woman?''

"Then I'll come back and kill you if Señorita Oliver is not here in one hour.'' There was a chill smile on Ki's face. *Comprende?*''

Murder was still shining in Murillo's eyes, but his voice was like the purring of a cat. "On second thought, it will be a pleasure to have your lady searched for. Pedro! On your feet! You and One-eye Gonzales look for Señorita Oliver.''

"Mucho gracias.'' Ki tipped his hat. "Your whole-hearted cooperation warms me without measure.'' And with that he turned and walked out the door.

Not a sound followed him. He moved on and mounted his horse, ignoring danger that might yet come from the cantina. Two men came out of the door and paused there in front of it long enough to roll and light cigarettes. One man was bearded, partly hiding a knife-scarred face; the other was swarthily dark, with a broad, fleshy nose and pockmarked skin. They had the depraved, vacant look of loafers or barflies who'd kill a man as quick as they'd kill an ant, not only without compunction, but almost without consciousness or thought.

Ki started riding toward the end of the cantina, aware

they were after him, sizing him up. He made sure his back was not to them, knowing they'd gun from behind if given the chance. How long he might last in Quevidas was a question that did not trouble him in the least. He would smoke it out with Murillo's bunch and take what came, good, bad, or indifferent.

Rounding the corner of the building, Ki kept more or less in shadow as he approached the pole and adobe horse sheds at the rear of the sprawling cantina. Reining in, his swinging left foot had no more than touched the ground before the ragged Mexican youth who had taken his horse last time came running over, grinning expectantly. Ki flipped him a dime.

"Ah, Don Americano!" The youth rubbed the coin and touched his tongue to it, testing counterfeit, then thrust it somewhere in his ragged pants. He reached for the reins, but Ki did not hand them over.

Instead, Ki drew more small change from his pocket and spun another ten-cent piece through the air. "Today, I look for a sorrel with a taffy mane."

The boy heard his words and backed away, eyes shifty. "I know no sorrel, Señor."

Ki spun him a third coin. "A sorrel with a taffy mane."

"I do not know. I swear—"

"The sorrel!" Ki's hand swept back, closing on the butt of his .44-40 pistol. "You saw it. Night before last. A señorita aboard a sorrel with a taffy mane. Where was she taken?"

"Nombre de Dios—me, povero—"

Ki did not draw, merely lifted the gun a trifle in its holster; much of the reason he had armed himself was for show, to intimidate. "Tell me!"

"P-perhaps away, out of Quevidas. From the cantina of Felipe Murillo. But I know nothing. I am but poor—"

"Sure. I never saw you before." Ki tossed him a silver dollar. *"Gracias.* It was worth it. It'll be worth five just like that one if you'll tell me where Luiz Zugate is."

140

"He come. He go. I do not know where he is right now, truly!" the boy exclaimed, staring wide-eyed at the dollar in his grimy hand. "And, and if I did, señor, it would be this." He dragged his forefinger across his throat to indicate the slash of a knife.

He was gone with that, leaping backward as if he expected a blow in spite of the dollar. Ki made no attempt to halt him. He knew these ragged urchins of the streets. That dollar would have its own chance to soften the youth. Ki felt that he might see him again, and as if the boy had not spoken to him at all, he strolled back to the plaza.

He stood there blinking in the sunlight for a moment, before he caught the bulky outlines of two men propped back in the deep shadow of a doorway at the other end of the old building. They were the pair who had watched him outside the cantina. Now they were waiting for him, that was a certainty.

Never one who hesitated to take a situation by the heels, Ki headed straight for them. They stiffened, each standing there with his thumbs hooked over heavy gunbelts, then turned and walked hastily away with furtive glances over their shoulders. Ki simply dogged them up around the side of the plaza, keeping close to them until he was near the end of the plaza diagonally opposite the cantina. They melted around a corner, into a dark slit of an alleyway between buildings. Ki was about to swing abruptly away when something flashed through the sunlight from a roof overhead.

A knife whizzed past him, just clearing his left shoulder. He heard its metallic clatter as it struck the cobblestones, and then the quiet was drowned out in a sudden long shriek of plummeting death.

It came from the man who was foolish enough to peer over the edge of the roof above Ki after he had sent his knife spinning down. His figure outlined itself up there against the brassy sky, as he stiffened outward, hands thrust blindly in front of him. Like a diver plunging into a pool, he came on down, a big lifeless thing that hit the plaza like a wet sponge. One of Ki's *shuriken* had caught him midway between his left eye and the bridge of his nose.

Something had misfired in the plans of the two gunmen Ki had followed. They were the lead-ons, the ones to bring Ki to the proper place for the slaughter. The man who had been on the roof had moved a moment before he had been supposed to swing into action, and the devil was to pay now.

The two gunmen made a foolish as well as fatal mistake. They whirled like snarling wolves in a trap. They tried to unholster their pistols when they should have flung on down the alley or dived into a doorway. Shots drowned out their savage burst of oaths as they faced Ki, for his throwing daggers impaled them as the barrels of their weapons cleared their holsters, and they triggered spasmodically while crumpling in blood-spurting death.

It was up and going now. All the tension and waiting had been cast out of the picture by the reverberating thunder of the guns. Yet the bullets from those final wild shots richochetted off the walls of the confining alley, and a slug grazed Ki's temple near the wound where lead and gunbutts had clipped him before. Still not over the effects of concussion, Ki went down to this knecs, shaking his head. For a moment he was out of the fight, addled, uncertain. Foggily he could hear other gunmen fast converging, drawn by the reports. It would have been the end of him if the loop of a rope had not hissed out of an alley doorway to close around his shoulders and yank him inside to safety.

"*Perdone, señor!*" a young voice apologized. "It is but me, Rojas, the amigo who help with your horse. Come, hurry! I know a way of escape from the mob surrounding you."

It was dark as it could be. A man could not see his hand before him, but Ki followed the boy along a narrow corridor that was like a tunnel boring deep within the building's interior. There was a taste of blood in his mouth, and a throbbing pain was wracking his head. He pulled his hat tighter to keep back the blood welling from his scalp wound, and blindly kept on in the darkness.

Ducking into an alcove, Rojas lifted a trapdoor in the wood floor. "Down the ladder, quick." Dazedly Ki started below, into a basement dimly lighted by a grease-dip on an old packing box. The boy, holding the door, said, "Señor, wait for me. I too wish to do something in this." Before Ki could respond, Rojas dropped the door and was gone.

The basement was a room the size of a small root cellar, its earthen walls patchworked with salvaged packing box tops and scrap lumber. Near the packing box table were a couple of rickity chairs, and in one corner was a home-made cot with a soiled USA blanket hanging half to the dirt floor. This must be Rojas' pitiful quarters, Ki surmised, though the rough yet tidy look of things seemed to indicate a woman's touch.

There also was a crudely built yet effective crossbar setup to block the trap door. Ki slid the bar in place, then sat on a chair and groggily wondered how dumb could he get, trusting Rojas. The kid was streetwise, no doubt aware that helping would probably earn him nothing but trouble—unless Murillo paid him for his trouble. Ki waited anyway, logic be damned. He was still resting, speculating how much Rojas would sell him out for, when a rapid step sounded above. Someone tugged at the trap door, then beat a fist on it. Revolver in hand, Ki padded over to keep close watch on the door and crossbar, figuring at the first sign of breakage, he'd fire through the floorboards.

A testy voice called, "Open up!"

"Evita!" Ki breathed her name with a sigh of dismay, recognizing the sharp tone of the cantina conchita. Quietly he climbed the ladder and craned listening at the door panel. He couldn't hear anything suspicious, no creaking of boots, no low breathing of men with her set to pounce.

"*Dese prisa*—get moving!" she snapped crossly. "Let me in!" Might as well, Ki supposed; after all, Rojas claimed the spitfire was his sister, so maybe he'd sent her for good reason. Warily he removed the bar and dived aside to cover the opening door.

Evita entered like a gust of wind, rebarring the door after her as she swept down the ladder, and flounced over to rail at Ki. "What kept you? Are you dead as you look? No? Don't tempt me, I think I could kill you myself!" Her eyes, however, contradicted her tongue.

"Don't bloody your hands. The hunt is on for me, isn't it?"

"*Bobo*—fool! They're out after me, too, due to you. Si, to your big fight, when you sided with me against Zugate, then seemed to leave with me. So they think we're together somehow, and threaten to take it out on me."

Evita faltered, regarding Ki, who was regarding her—in her skimpy frock, a pink shirtlike *baton*, washworn and faded to the opacity of gauze, clinging almost translucent to her lush breasts and bottom. Glaring at Ki, she reared stiffly indignant—which only drew the cloth tighter and hiked the hem, revealing she wore nothing beneath her gossamer *baton*, while exhibiting long legs from her bare feet to the swell of her thighs. Ki grinned appreciatively. She fixed him with a regal glower and plated her fists on her hips. "Never mind me. Did Rojas bring you here?"

"Squawk any louder, you'll bring everybody else here."

"There's not enough brains between you two," she hissed, "to make a pimple on a fly! Why didn't you stay away when you had the chance?"

"I'm not finished in Quevidas," Ki said stubbornly.

"You're so finished the buzzards are alightin' on the roof," she retorted fiercely, then stared tight-lipped at Ki, slowly cooling, some of her wildness draining away. Finally, allowing, "Even a condemned man deserves to be cared for," she gently removed Ki's blood-soaked hat to examine his scalp wound.

As blood held by the hat rivuleted down his face, Ki hastily leaned forward so the flow dripped to the floor from his nose and chin. Evita pawed through Rojas' effects and found a few remnants of clothing to use for bandaging. The last wound proved to be a clean furrow along his temple just above his ear.

"Just creased—nothing broken," she assured him, while she concentrated on probing his skullbone with sensitive fingers. Her body kept brushing against him, and when she began bandaging him around front, she leaned so close that her nipples poked him in the eyes. Che-rist! Never mind her nevermind, Ki thought, blinking, measuring her breasts' impressive roundness and the shadowed delta of her svelte loins. . . . The bandage, made of torn strips of clothing tied end to end, was not quite long enough. Evita promptly ripped a strip from around the hem of her *baton* and deftly finished bandaging . . . and Ki groaned softly, thinking her shortened frock might as well be a *yukata*, a small, thin body sheet which served as a boudoir kimono. . . .

"There, that's as good as I can snug it," she said, eyeing her handiwork. "I should snug it around your neck. You're a danger, Señor Ki, a danger."

He said nothing, feeling stirrings, thinking *she* was the danger.

She said, "Don't sit there and try to look stupid. You don't fool me a bit. Inside, you must be a wonderful man. You knew I am . . . what I am, yet you felt I was worth defending against many. I heard a word, no more, that they harm another woman now, and at great peril you come back to this renegade sanctuary." She stroked a finger shakily down one side of his cheek. "I don't believe you are a desperado. You are a killer, but you aren't that kind of killer, the Zugate kind. You couldn't be."

Ki did not respond at once. Words were secondary; he felt the force of a sudden chemistry between them. *Of all the damn times and places,* he thought, standing up, giving her a new appraisal. She stood close to him, her head turned facing him gravely, and her eyes gripped his. Ki knew, by her face, that she wanted his kiss; there was no mistake about that. But with Rojas due momentarily, and the whole town liable to drop in at any time, he wouldn't be courting a dame, he'd be courting danger and maybe disaster. Even as he was telling hiself this, agreeing with everything he advised, he was slipping his hand around behind her and drawing her forward. Her eyes widened, her breathing quickened, and for a moment she pushed her palms against his chest, drawing back. But her lips parted slowly and the thrust of her hands relaxed; her arms went around him and there was sudden urgency in her hungry kiss.

Their kiss grew more demanding, and they embraced almost savagely, the fires mounting in them. Slowly, then, while keeping pressed against Ki, Evita eased down to sit in his chair, her hands gliding along her chest and abdomen and thighs. Her curious fingers found the bulge of his growing erection and traveled its length, and she made a whimpering sound in her throat as she traced his thickening column, while her other hand nimbly untied his rope belt and unbuttoned his fly. Hurriedly she tugged his jeans down and grasped his exposed shaft.

"Ahh, *estupendo* . . ." She licked her lips.

Ki rubbed a hand through her hair. "Your dress . . ."

She shook her head. "I know. It's better when you're naked, but my brother or someone else might come along; You never can tell." Her eyes closed and she bent closer. "You stay dressed, too." Her pink tongue ran moistly around the full lips of her mouth, then fluted out to lick the crown of his manhood. She seemed to taste him, to see if she liked him, then fitted her mouth over to swallow him whole.

Her teeth scraped along his aching girth as she tightened her lips and began a tentative sucking motion. Her hands stroked his buttocks and cupped his scrotum, gently squeezing, while she bobbed her mouth back and forth. Ki

146

gasped and watched, his eyes flaring as she sucked harder and absorbed more of his flesh into her clasping mouth, his hips beginning to move in concert, his groin boiling, threatening to spill over. He fought to hold back, the sensations feeling exquisite . . . until without warning, she released him and lifted her head.

"First *de entremés*—the hors d'oeuvre, now *la entrada*—the entrée," she said smiling.

Sensuously she stood up and turned her back to him, hiking the remaining bottom of her *baton* up and tucking it around her waist, baring herself from her feet to her opulent buttocks. Leaning over the packing crate table, she positioned herself with her head cradled in her arms.

"*Ahora*," she cooed, "Now, right now . . ."

Ki ran his hands across her naked cheeks and between her inner thighs, feeling the moisture of her anticipation, then moved deeper inside the lips of her cleft, one finger dipping easily into tight, slippery head. She moaned, her inner muscles contracting in a rhythmic, squeezing pulse around his finger. Then feeling Ki pressing against her, she arched to reach and clasp his hardness, guiding it to replace his finger in her warm sheath.

Ki slid inside her a long way before he realized how tight she was. He looked down at her trembling hunched figure and lanced deeper into her, and it seemed he could almost feel the very depth of her. He began to pump hard then, and she seemed to grow even tighter around him, until every time he would thrust into her, she would gasp, shuddering, from the impact. Yet eagerly she undulated her buttocks back against him, greedy for more. There was nothing timid or gentle by their union, Ki thought, as he plunged to the hilt in her gripping hot depths.

"*Más, más* . . . More, more . . ."

Her thighs pistoned into tempo with his strokes, and her inner muscles clasped him as if she would hold him forever. Her gasps became moans, soulful and prolonged, and she sunk her mouth into her arm in an attempt to keep from screaming in a cascade of incoherent emotion. She was consumed by the fire in her that was mounting like a holocaust, devouring everything but the hunger to have Ki charge on, to have him finish what she had begun.

"*Venga rápido*—come quickly!" she moaned. "*Venga! Venga!*"

Her pleading choked off in a staccato sputtering as she shuddered convulsively in orgasm. Ki, yielding to his own burgeoning climax, speared forward simultaneously, embedding and ejaculating deep inside her.

They collapsed in a satiated heap, Evita sprawling on the packing box beneath Ki's spent form. For a while they stayed pinned that way, savoring the fulfillment of their pressing need. When at last Ki withdrew from her, Evita straightened on wobbly legs and brushed out her frock, smiling contentedly from a peculiarly satisfying ache.

"I knew there was some reason not to kill you," she purred.

Ki stared slackly. "What d'you mean, not kill me? You just did. . . ."

Not many minutes later Rojas arrived back. He stumbled down the ladder, burdened by two heavy leather strap pouches, a worn shellbelt whose holster held an elderly Spiller & Burr percussion pistol, and a second, even older firearm that was the clumsiest-looking weapon Ki had ever seen. It was more than a gun. It was an *escopeta*, a long-barreled, hand-crafted shotgun with a bore that seemed like the mouth of a cannon.

"A mob hides in the cantina stables, señor, where you left your horse. They're so sure of themselves. Come, we will take to the roofs," the boy urged Ki, anxious to head out.

"Sí, it's your only way," Evita agreed. "Give me the pistol."

She and Ki, of course, gave no hint of any tomfoolery. But with that uncanny sense of younger brothers, Rojas

148

caught on and started smirking as he handed his sister the shellbelt. "I might've known."

"You know nothing, and don't be smart about it," she retorted, buckling on the cumbersome gunrig. To Ki, it looked incongruous around her wispily clad waist, but firing that piece— or the antique shotgun—was no joke, unless you cared to die laughing. Telling him, "Go now. Afterward, I go my way," Evita gave Ki a peck on the cheek. "May your aim keep true, and may their aim remain as bad as it has been."

Ki helped Rojas tote the *escopeta* up through the trap-door. The alcove and corridor beyond were still pitch black, but he followed the boy more easily this time, guided by the *escopeta* bumping along the walls. Then his feet stubbed the bottom step of a steep flight of stairs. As they ascended a crack of light showed overhead.

"The roof, señor," Rojas whispered. "Take care."

Now, that Ki found funny in an ironic way. He wasn't here to take care, but to disrupt, to distract, to make a rabble-rousing target. Hit, ram, tear the shit out.

It was like that when he once reached the roof. A gang on a roof across the alley opened up at him. Immediately he returned fire, ready as he burst into view with both .44-40 Colts, having brought the spare from his saddle holster. The gang began scattering, the lead flying into them sending them stumbling and falling, colliding with one another, a wild scramble to get out of the way.

"From roof to roof you may go now, señor," Rojas encouraged.

It sounded simple enough, but it was not. Gunmen were crowding to a roof ahead of him. They snap-triggered at him in a vain attempt to substitute speed for accuracy, but at ranges over twenty feet, it wasn't the first bullet fired that mattered, so much as the first bullet to hit home. Bunched jostling, they offered much more home to hit than Ki did. As well, the seven-and-a-half-inch barrels of his Colts were longer, heavier than most all of their pistol barrels, giving less kickback and better aim, making for greater accuracy. He drove the men back with a rain of bullets, ignoring their fireworks blazing close around, holding the revolver he was shooting chest-high and level, and the second revolver lax and pointed down, to take over firing when the other clicked empty.

Rojas did the reloading as they advanced, trading revolvers, picking Ki's pockets for ammunition with sticky-fingered skill. The strap pouches he toted over his shoulder, and he hung on to the *escopeta* bulldoggedly, though he had yet to set it off.

"My grandfather's," Rojas explained when a lull came in the firing. "I wish to turn it loose by the front door of the cantina and see the roof fall. Felipe Murillo, he lets Zugate beat Evita near to death there. Me, he has worked for weeks, and my only pay has been slaps and kicks and threats to slice off my *pene* if I failed him. I pay him now a bang-up surprise."

"Well, whatever happens, Murillo has to live to tell us what he did with the woman," Ki said, "the woman on the sorrel with the taffy mane."

"*Muy bien.* Then I slice off his *pene* so he do it no more."

Ki wouldn't put it past the whelp to do just that, if given the chance. They were getting close to the cantina at last. Traveling over roof after roof with Rojas showing him the way, Ki came to a place where he could see the big cantina. He was not watching the youth when Rojas fired.

Rojas merely laid his old shoulder cannon on the edge of a roof, took careful aim, and pulled the trigger with both hands. He heeled over backward as if a mule had kicked him. And down below, diagonally across an alleyway bordering the plaza, there was a showering and crashing of glass, the smashing of chairs, and the rush of booted feet. Rojas sat up and yelled with triumph.

Ki left him there as he climbed down from the roof, and then angled across the lane with gunshots blistering the air around him. He banged into the front doors of the cantina. In dust-fogged light stood Murillo, hunched now like a ferret in front of the bar, his gimlet eyes staring at a dead man on the floor, and a wreckage of bloody splinters that had been a heavy plank before Rojas' heavy charge of shot and cut slugs of lead had torn through the door.

"Reach, Felipe!" Ki yelled a warning to the bandido chief, but Murillo did not heed it. He dived toward the foot of the bar, bawling, "Shoot!" as his hand swung for the double-barreled pistol in his sash. "Shoot him!"

Ki took a long stride, reversing the Colt in his right hand, stretched across the bar and brought the pistol butt down. It hit Murillo on the skull with the sound heard in a slaughterhouse, when a steer was brained with a maul. The double-pistol thudded to the earthen floor, followed by Murillo in a dead heap.

The bar was next, falling fast. Shabbily built, weakened by tough times and dryrot, it broke under the strain of Ki lunging to hit Murillo. The counter split loose from its floor brace and tilted over, Ki rolling with it. Paneling and shelves pulled apart, collapsing in pieces like a house of cards and burying Murillo under the debris.

Ki came out of his roll in a low dive. He had figured on dropping behind the bar, to use it for cover, but that idea was shot to hell and he was bound to be, too, in another second. But not even the drawn guns of the bandidos in the cantina were quick enough to down him, before a long black barrel rammed through the doorway. Rojas' hell-scattering shotgun let out one more roar and kicked the youth into insensibility, its heavy charge splitting the end of the barrel and cutting three men into a mass of bloody ribbons.

The rest was hell with the lights out. Short, jabbing gashes of flames jerked at each other. Lamps were knocked out. Tables crashed, chairs splintered into wreckage. Men went down, sobbing and cursing, some against the wall,

151

some into the middle of the floor or spilling over the tables.

Abruptly Ki realized that he was not doing all the shooting. Bullets were coming in at the windows and from the back door. Jessie, Wade Duval, Frost, and Yarbrough, even Evita were in this thing, taking a quick, hot part in it. As hands flung up and gunmen started surrendering, the noise of the shooting died away, and Ki found himself standing there, the only man in the cantina with guns in his hand.

Then, out of the shade in back of the cantina came Jessie. Behind her streamed the others, Evita standing poised for a moment at the threshold and then fleeing into Ki's arms.

"You can count on it," Jessie began with mock exasperation. "If there's a lady within fifty miles—"

"Ki played 'er right," Duval cut in, grinning, and addressed Ki. "Your friend caught us creeping into Quevidas, and near shot our heads off before we convinced her we're with you. Then she sure was a help sneaking us here to the cantina. That was a big risk you took, setting yourself up as a decoy, flushing out the enemy. You waited until they was all set an' started, and then you banged in. We was all lying back, waitin'."

Vaughn Yarbrough nodded. "And the vultures are gonna have some damn tough eating tonight."

★
Chapter 11

The surviving gunmen were herded into the cantina cellar for safekeeping. Evita left, helping her brother back to his cellar quarters. Felipe Murillo was unearthed from beneath the rubble of the bar, gasping from pain, eyeballs rolled focusing on his double-gun. He staggered upright, retreated a pace.

The gun lay at Jessie's feet. She booted it out of temptation's way, her stern eyes warning against any foolhardy move. "You're riding with us, Murillo. We're after Prudence Oliver."

Murillo managed a cold, albeit shaken, smile. "You are not the law in *Mejico*, Señorita Starbuck. I do not have to obey and go with you."

"Now, that's a good point. We're not figuring on such niceties as arrest. You and Luiz Zugate are holding Miss Oliver a prisoner. We mean to get her back. If you and Zugate and more of your men get hurt, it can't be helped."

"Speaking of Zugate," Ki added, "where is he? He ought to be here."

"I know nothing," Murillo muttered, shrugging.

Ki frowned. "I'll check if Zugate's hiding in Quevidas."

"Let me help," Leo Frost offered. "We'll tear the place apart."

The two men left the cantina and their footsteps faded away. They would be an hour or more searching the town, Jessie estimated, turning back to Murillo.

Murillo looked sullen and uncertain, his beady eyes darting from Jessie to Duval and Yarbrough. "I . . . I shall call the Rurales," he bluffed.

"Sure, after the Mashed-O gets through with your hide," Jessie replied. "Then you can yell your head off. But be dead sure you can explain Miss Oliver's abduction, your hideout in the hills with Zugate, a lot of stolen cattle and a murder or two."

"I'd druther the rat explains now." Duval was grinding fist against palm, his eyes burning like coals in his rigid face. "He has the sort of neck that should produce a long, strong voice, but I haven't heard it."

Murillo bared his teeth like a wolf at bay. "I've nothing to tell."

"Your problem is," Duval told Murillo, "your neck is bent, putting kinks in the root of your tongue. It ought to be straightened out. Yeah, I reckon perhaps if your neck was given a stretch at the end of a rope, it just might loosen your tongue." He turned toward the door. "I'll fetch my lariat."

"Don't!" snapped a harsh voice behind Jessie, the order punctuated with the click of a gunhammer. "It's gone far enough. Reach!"

Jessie whirled as Wade Duval froze.

Vaughn Yarbrough stood with his revolver covering them, his muddy eyes glinting and his thin lips twisting sardonically. "Felipe, pull their fangs. They know too

154

much to stay alive. Get your boys out of the cellar, and we'll ride these folks out of Quevidas, pronto."

Jessie slowly raised her hands. "So you're the traitor on the Mashed-O . . ." she breathed softly.

Ki and Leo Frost duly tore Quevidas apart. Hunting from hovel to hovel through dust, disorder, and squalor, they met with various protests and assorted expletives, but they paid no attention. A 'breed Indian tried for a knife, but Frost's lashing fists smashed the man against the wall; he slept through the remainder of the search.

They found no trace of Luiz Zugate. Not surprisingly, no one admitted to having seen Zugate, to knowing anything at all about him. At last, having progressed from one end of the settlement to the other, they were forced to give up and return in disgust to the cantina. Vaughn Yarbrough was calmly waiting for them there, but Jessie, Wade Duval, and the vicious cantina owner were gone.

"Miz Starbuck and Duval left already with that Murillo jasper. They went on ahead to meet Sweetwater an' the boys over at the hills, like we planned."

"Why didn't they wait for us?" Ki asked.

"Hell, you got me. Miz Starbuck said to hang tight till you guys showed, and that's good enough for me." Yarbrough paused, casting a dark look at the locked cellar door, through which groans and babbles of the imprisoned bandidos could be heard. "Let 'em rot. We'll come back later with the boys and collect 'em. Right now I reckon we'd better hit leather if we're going to catch up."

Ki glanced at Leo Frost as if for his opinion, but the mine superintendent merely shrugged and started for the door. When they gathered their horses, Ki watched Yarbrough as he swung into the saddle. The muddy eyes divulged nothing, nor was there anything suspicious in the dour foreman's actions as they rode out of Quevidas. Still, Ki didn't cotton to the feel of things. . . .

•   •   •

Felipe Murillo had moved swiftly when Yarbrough had gotten the drop on Jessie and Wade Duval. The Mexican bandido chief appropriated their revolvers, then located some rawhide cord and lashed their wrists tightly behind them.

"It is a mistake you have made, no? Felipe Murillo, he not talk. You talk—to Luiz Zugate, gringos."

Coldly ignoring Murillo, Jessie glared at Vaughn Yarbrough. "They don't come lower than you, selling out your ranch, your own family relatives who took you in."

"T'was never my ranch, my crew, and my kin's never let me forget it." Yarbrough peeled his lips in a nasty, mirthless grin. "Wal, the days of me being the poor relation slaving for them, doing the work of three hands for one hand's begrudged pay, are over. Now I'll have the Mashed-O for mine."

"First you have Señors Ki and Frost to lead from here," Murillo directed Yarbrough. "To lull suspicions, I'll leave my men in the cellar until you go, and then we'll take this pair to Zugate."

Jessie's face darkened, and Duval strained his muscles at the bonds, to no avail. Murillo and Yarbrough shoved them toward the rear door, and they were half pushed to the stables, where they were hidden in a dank, smelly tack shed. Yarbrough went back to the cantina, while Murillo waited with the prisoners.

Duval swore low and luridly. "So Yarbrough's the polecat in this, is he?"

"One of them," Jessie replied absently, peering through chinks in the boards at the adjacent stables. "Not the big'un, or the one who caught Pru."

"Silencio!" Murillo snarled, enforcing his order by pressing the twin muzzles of his recovered pistol against Duval's ear.

Soon Jessie caught sight of Ki coming from the direction of the cantina. She wanted to yell, but was convinced Murillo would splatter Duval's brains all over the tack shed at the first sound out of either of them. She had to watch helplessly as Ki collected his horse, then left with Frost and Yarbrough to get their mounts. Her eyes grew bleak. Apparently the traitorous foreman planned to kill his companions once away from town, and should he do so, Jessie pledged to track him down and blast him to the hell he so richly deserved.

Murillo chuckled. "*Bueno.* Now we release my *much-achos.*"

Minutes later a handful of re-armed bandidos streamed out of the cantina to saddle up horses, sunlight reflecting off rifle barrels. The two captives were hoisted aboard their mounts and Murillo led the way out of Quevidas. The small cavalcade set a swift pace toward the hills along a circuitous route that hid them from view.

There was no chance of escape, but Jessie bided her time, hoping. She jerked when she heard a faint shot, followed immediately by a second. That would be Yarbrough making his drygulch move. Murillo turned with a diabolical smile.

"You are beaten, Señorita Starbuck. Your amigo is dead, Señorita Oliver is our prisoner, and soon you shall see us kill the Mashed-O gringos. Quivedas was a ver' bad visit for you, *no es verdad . . . ?*"

In the meantime Ki had been feeling little prickles of warning chase down his spine as he rode along with Leo Frost and Vaughn Yarbrough. They had been hitting a brisk pace and the distant hills were rapidly growing nearer, every stretch of the way seeming to him like riding through a miles-long den of rattlers. Occasionally he threw a glance at his companions, who rode hard, their eyes on the hills. His concern was much closer, aware at any moment the brush might burst fire and bullets. He studied every flanking knoll, scanned every wall of chaparral and clump of mesquite, every muscle tense with expectation.

But mile after mile passed, and nothing happened. The

157

horses clacked along, little trails of dust rising behind them. Presently they came upon a boulder-hedged pocket clearing, where Leo Frost reined in, calling a halt.

"Got to take a piss," he declared, dismounting.

Ki and Yarbrough stepped down. Smoking a quick-rolled quirly, Yarbrough squinted toward the yonder hills, then looked at Ki. "Still no sign of Duval and Miz Starbuck up ahead. Maybe they got lost. The crew might be hard to spot in the folds of land at the base of those hills."

A few feet away Frost finished and turned with a satisfied grunt.

Now Yarbrough took the cigarette stub casually from his mouth and dropped it on the ground. In the same careless motion, he put out his foot and stamped on it. It was a common, natural action. Except that he used his left hand. His right hand swung back to his holster and grasped his pistol butt.

"Hey!" Frost stabbed to draw, but the foreman was quicker. Before Frost touched palm to revolver, Yarbrough had his weapon up, finger squeezing to fire.

The foreman was quicker, all right, but Ki was quickest. He twisted aside with a tigerish lunge, knowing that a trap had been sprung; a snap-wristed throwing dagger flashed straight through the air and lanced into Yarbrough's right forearm, stabbing deep through muscle and ligament. It plunged Yarbrough off balance. Triggering inadvertently, he drilled a gaping hole through his right boot and shattered his foot. Howling, reeling, he dropped to his knees—

Ki aimed another dagger—

And Frost shot to kill. Yarbrough went over and back.

There were the two thunderous reverberations, then a long moment of utter silence while Ki and Frost stared at Yarbrough and each other.

"Why, he was fixing to kill us," Frost said, after a deep breath.

"Money paid has to be earned."

"Just shoot us like we was empty beer bottles on a

fencepost.'' Frost, slowly reholstering, shook his head. "I don't know what the play's about, but I want to tell you something, Ki. In all my borned days I never saw knifery as fast as yours.''

"If you'd been some of the places I've been," Ki said evenly, "and seen some of the men I've seen, you'd have seen faster." Then he asked, "What's happened to Jessie and Wade Duval?''

"Something nasty, I suspect. P'raps we best return to Quevidas.''

Ki rubbed an earlobe and looked reflectively at the foreman's body. "I doubt we'd find them still there. Yarbrough was too much at ease when we got back to the cantina. No, I've a hunch that they've been taken to Luiz Zugate.''

"Why?''

"Hostages, maybe. C'mon, let's get to the Mashed-O crew.''

Frost pointed to Yarbrough. "Him?''

"We'll bring him along. Give them something to chew on.''

They tied Yarbrough crosswise over his saddle like a sack of feed. With grim-visaged urgency, then, the two men began leading the corpse-laden horse toward the hills and the help of the Mashed-O. . . .

Jessie had refused to answer Murillo's taunting question, and the little man spurred to the head of his motley bunch. The ridges came closer, and they rode directly into a gulch that led deeper, higher into the windswept hills.

As the peaks closed around them, the rocky path became single-file. From a ridge above, a lookout shouted out. Murillo and his bandidos gave an answering halloo and moved on, angling toward an extremely narrow cleft in the tall stone walls. Beyond, the path wound upward in a steepening ascent, topped a rise, and descended the far slope into a *vallecito*, a little cup of a valley.

Jessie saw the tents and huts of the bandits, the stout corral and the cattle that grazed on meager tufts of grass growing between the stones. She didn't doubt but what the herd bore the Mashed-O brand. The camp seemed filled with bandidos who clustered around the prisoners as they were helped from the saddle and led away. Rough hands thrust them into a sort of cave-hut, made by roofing a natural crevasse with timber and flat slabs of shale. Their bonds were cut and the heavy plank door was slammed shut.

A few streaks of sunlight fanned through the cracks in the door, piercing the gloom just enough to see by. Jessie listened at the door while she rubbed the circulation back in her arms. Discounting the noise of Wade Duval angrily pacing around the small confines, she heard only normal camp sounds and then a closer rustle of someone on guard. Finally she straightened up.

"Take things a little easier, Wade," she advised. "Maybe later we'll use some of that energy."

Duval halted, facing her sharply. "How? When? We're unarmed, caught in the trap Yarbrough set for us, simple as that."

"No, there's more to it," she said, "so there's more to go wrong." They were not entirely unarmed, either, Jessie still possessing the derringer hidden behind her belt buckle. She held off mentioning it, though, afraid it would only prod Duval more impatient and reckless. "Keep alert for a chance to escape, but don't show it. Keep them lazy and unalert. And when the time comes, we'll act."

Duval strode back and forth for a few more minutes before he realized the wisdom of Jessie's advice and settled down, his back to the wall. Time passed, marked only by the slow movement of the bars of sunlight through the door. The afternoon was far along when noises outside made the two prisoners stiffen. Shrill voices sputtered excited Spanish. Orders snapped and they heard the hasty

160

thump of feet as bandidos ran toward the corrals. Abruptly the door swung open.

Luiz Zugate's bulk stood framed in the doorway. Close beside him Murillo grinned evilly. Just behind them Jessie had a glimpse of Prudence Oliver's drawn face, while in the background hovered Brazos Chaldeen.

"Careful, hombre!" Zugate warned, leveling his revolver as Duval sprang to his feet. "The señorita, she would not like to see blood."

He stepped aside and Murillo pushed Prudence in with a tight grip on her arm. There the girl was forced to stand, slim and boyish in denims and broad-brimmed hat, pale with fright but apparently unharmed.

"We leave Señorita Oliver in your company, so one man he can guard all of you. Brazos Chaldeen will see you do not stray far," Murillo said, his eyes hard and glittery. "The Mashed-O has found our pass into the hills here, but it will do them no good. We ride now, I and my brave *compañeros*, and we will set a welcome for them. It shall also be their good-bye."

"Then what?" Jessie demanded.

"Then we do what we wish." Murillo stroked Prudence's hair and widened his malevolent grin. "Ah, the love she's wonderful!"

Hot-headed Duval made a lunge. "Why, you—!"

With a barking laugh, Murillo flung Prudence at Duval and sent them both tumbling in a tangle. *"Hasta la vista,"* he intoned mockingly, backing out, and Zugate slammed the door. The clack of a lock was heard. Murillo growled orders to Brazos Chaldeen, and then the three in the little hut heard him walk away with Zugate. In a few moments the earth shook with the pounding of many hooves. The bandidos were riding off to crush the Mashed-O.

Prudence was appalled when briefed on the facts, especially about her cousin's perfidity. "Lord, I never figured Vaughn for a double-crosser."

161

"Yarbrough's a dog," Wade Duval declared. "A scurvied dog, biting the hand that fed it."

"As well as slipping a ring on your hand, Pru," Jessie noted.

"Marry him!" Prudence made a face. "I never figured on a lot of things."

"Well, I don't think your foreman's figured things through," Jessie said. "He's figured his price for selling you out is controlling the Mashed-O, becoming his own boss again. But my hunch is he'll end up a captive underling like Brazos Chaldeen."

That idea led Jessie to consider Chaldeen himself. Prudence and Duval went on discussing the circumstances, Duval with a sappy expression on his face, and Pru looking at him in a fascinated way—almost a shameless stare. Though Duval had glimpsed Pru once or twice in Ingot, this was the first they had met, and if the situation weren't so serious, Jessie would've been bemused by how they seemed to take to each other. Instead she impatiently tested the door. Someone had to warn the Mashed-O crew— and they were locked in and guarded, set to be killed.

Daylight was waning when Jessie heard Chaldeen just outside the door. She placed her lips close to a wide crack. "You made a couple of bad moves, Brazos, to Abilene and then the Big Bend. Don't make a worse move now that'll send you to the gallows."

There was a silence that held so long Jessie wondered if the rustler had heard her. Then the key rattled in the lock and the door swung open. Chaldeen entered the gloomy hut, revolver in hand.

"What d'you know about Abilene and here?" he demanded.

"A bellyful. I know you went on the lam, your gang smashed, and thought you could start over clean. I know you got tripped up by other men with tight 'lass ropes and no heart." Jessie stood straight, eyes showing no fear.

162

Only defiance. "I know the deal is to drill us and dump our bodies somewhere."

"Aw'ri', then you know I'm hogtied without much choice. And I sure's hell know you'd send me to hang if you caught me operating on the other side of the Rio. Well, you're caught on this side. Sauce for the gander, hey?"

She gave a scornful smile. "Do you shoot women in Texas?"

"I do what I have to," Chaldeen contended, though his lips twisted down as if in distaste, and his eyes seemed restive and brooding. "I don't crave to, mind. Can't say I cater to the notion of stealing females, neither."

"It's all the same to those butchers you ride with. Don't kid yourself, Brazos, they'll turn on you. They've already killed Mad Knecht."

"Mad? Dead?" Chaldeen looked jarred.

"They neglected to tell you, did they? Yesterday Ki and I stopped by your place and met with gunfire from some of Zugate's boys. They ran out on Knecht, but snuck back and cold-bloodedly knifed him before he could talk."

"No, you're lying—"

"I'm a Starbuck, not a rustler."

"Ah-so."

"Or a bandido the likes of Zugate and Murillo. Don't take it as an unfailing rule, but generally you can go farther on a Starbuck's word than you can on the word of a bandido."

Brazos Chaldeen stood silent, looking hot and bothered and vicious. When he spoke, he pointed his revolver and pantomimed a shot. "I ought to do it."

"But you won't."

"Reckon not. Me and Mad were sidekicks. He stuck with me in my trouble. Ain't nobody can stab him and not answer to me. P'raps that don't bring us on the same side, exactly, but I can't be holding you while hunting them for

163

Mad's killing. Ride out of here right now, all of you, afore I sober to my senses."

They didn't need a second invite.

By now the sun was down, the *vallecito* was thick with shadow, although the high crests were still bright and clear. By lamplight Brazos showed them where their gear had been stowed in another hut, and they hastened to rope and saddle their horses in the corral. Chaldeen was waiting when they started to leave, handing up cartridges and then their weapons, empty.

"We're mighty obliged, Mr. Chaldeen," Prudence said, accepting her pistol and saddle carbine. "Why not ride with us?"

"Not me, ma'am. I'm in too deep. I mean to skin me one or two hides in the neighborhood and then I'm striking south. Ain't coming back, ever. Miz Starbuck can give you an earful of particulars."

"Not me, Brazos," Jessie responded, smiling a little. "I've forgotten all about you, and I'll do my best that no one else remembers, much less wants you."

"Lady, you'll wind up queen of Texas someday, or maybe we'll all wind up dead." Chaldeen laughed, the old, cynical jerk of his shoulders, but this time with a touch of admiration. "Go on, you're wasting time. Back-trail it the way Murillo brung you in. Be plumb careful, though, 'cause Zugate's liable to be holed in the rocks around by that break in the canyon wall. *Adiós*, pass my regards to the Rio Grande."

Jessie watched the rustler fade away into the murky dusk. Her voice was low, barely audible to Pru and Duval alongside her. "A good man who paid dear for bad times. *Vaya con Dios, amigo.* . . ."

Earlier that evening, when sunset was inflaming the hills and searing the desert floor, Ki and Leo Frost reached the Mashed-O camp. While they loosened the ropes holding Vaughn Yarbrough, the crew pressed close around them,

seeming stunned at the sight of their renegade foreman—
stunned and angry as Frost explained what had happened.

"Ain't possible," Sweetwater growled agog. "I can't believe it."

"Waddie, the lead he aimed our way was damned real," Frost insisted. "Besides, Miz Starbuck and my office manager, Duval, have disappeared. Those raiders have took 'em, for a fact."

A hand cussed. "Shit, they could've took 'em anywhere."

"Strikes me they'd want to coop all their captives together," Ki pointed out. "Since Miss Pru's not in Quevidas, she's most likely held up at Zugate's hideout. I'd venture that's where Murillo has taken Jessie and Duval."

"They couldn've gotten up into these hills any number of ways other'n the cow track we're followin'," Sweetwater observed grimly. "Well, we'll keep on goin' the way we're followin', an' sooner or later we'll flush 'em out."

Another cowpoke spoke up, cautioning. "They'll be on the lookout, I betcha, and lay in ambush for us if we was to go after 'em."

He earned an angry rebuke from Sweetwater: "If they is or if the ain't, I don't give a rat's ass so long as I can line my sights on them gal-nappers. Now you can figure your own trail, Rogers. I hope it goes with the Mashed-O, but I ain't wasting time if it don't."

"Rogers ain't yellow for bein' wary," Leo Frost countered. "No telling how many bandidos we may find ourselves up against. Big Nick Tualatin has had time to round up a bunch of men by now, and I think I ought to go fetch them. If we don't need them after all, no harm done. But if we do . . . well, with two ladies' lives in peril, I'd hate to take any more risk than we have to."

Ki gave Frost a questioning glance, but the crew chorused their support. Sweetwater said, "You'd better keep out of sight on your way back to Ingot, Mr. Frost. You don't want to chance running into owlhoots."

Frost nodded as he rolled a quirly. "I know my way

165

through these hills pretty well,'' he assured them, lighting up. "I'll be back with Big Nick and our miners soon as possible.''

After the mine superintendent had ridden off, the Mashed-O buried Vaughn Yarbrough. No one mourned his death. They raised no crude wooden marker above him but only piled stones on his grave to keep the animals out. Then the men examined their weapons, ate a quick meal, saddled, and mounted.

The cattle trail entered a vast canyon that lay like a gaping mouth in the craggy face of the hills. From the start the canyon was narrow, with long and fairly steep banks spottily grown with manzanita and other chaparral. Then it began to squeeze in further, while it wound and twisted up through the hills, apparently following the tortuous course of some prehistoric river.

The Mashed-O was deep in the canyon when night closed down. More than ever Ki strained to scan the trail and slopes ahead, and spotted the thin cleft that broke off the main canyon, his eyes ranging upward to the rimrock. He saw no movement, heard no sound. In a few more minutes they came to the side draw, covered with darkness, the canyon pathway continuing on to lose itself among the shadowed barriers of stone. Ki called a halt, the men gathering round.

"I've a hunch the rustlers may've cut up here. Let's take a gander.''

A half-dozen riders joined Ki in scouting the cleft. Five minutes later they were back with the main bunch, one of the riders reporting, "There's lots of droppings and puddles of piss. No question our herd went up thataway.''

"We'll go ahead, but take it slow,'' Ki warned. "Spread out and some of you hug the walls. Keep your rifles handy and your eyes sharp.''

Into the crooked black cleft they snaked, climbing the steepening trail, peering for ambushes, the night quiet like a hushed yet vibrant warning to their suspicious ears. . . .

166

Suddenly the cleft was lashed with gunfire. All along the rim tongues of flame stabbed down toward the bunched Mashed-O crew. A rider next to Ki choked on his own blood and slid from the saddle. A horse screamed and plunged wildly, maddened by a burning slug.

"Hug the walls!" Ki yelled. "Climb!"

The crew scattered. The merciless fire from above continued to pour down, the whining bullets seeking out dodging bodies. Another man howled; his cry ended in a frightful gurgle. Ki and Sweetwater hit the ground together and hugged the protecting rocks, lead striking close and flinging stone fragments at their faces. The others, with bandido slugs whining about their ears, were not slow to hunt cover, either, immediately digging in and beginning to return fire.

Sweetwater started triggering and levering as fast as he could. Emptying his carbine, Ki shifted aside to reload, and as he glanced over to see how the others were doing, a lead chunk drilled into the earth where he'd just been. Twisting around, Ki shouldered his carbine and surveyed the rim.

The cleft resounded with crackling gunfire, blood-curdling screams, and the squeals of frightened horses. Calmly Ki ignored the melee around him, concentrating on the splintery facade of that rimrock, and his patience paid off. Spying the black form of a man in a wide-brimmed sombrero moving stealthily out from one niche and starting toward another, Ki sighted carefully before triggering. The man jerked, then tumbled over the edge,

Bullets smashed close around. The darkness offered some protection to both ambushers and defenders, but Ki knew that with the coming of daylight the Mashed-O would find itself pinned in a deadly trap.

"We've got to get around behind them!" he shouted to Sweetwater above the roar of guns. "Up there." He pointed toward a fault in one face of the cleft, which formed a steep but not impossible slope to the rim.

"I'm game. It ain't no fun here."

They slipped out along the bank, its crevices and cracks protecting them somewhat from the gunshots whipping and whining about them. At any instant, however, one of the bandidos could get their range or get lucky and plug them. The crew, catching their cautious ascent, realized what they were attempting and responded with increased barrages. The very noise of the exchange helped as well to cover their slow progress. As they neared the rimrocks and crept along a series of thin, angular ledges, they glimpsed dim figures crawl over the brow and scurry down toward them. The bandit leader was sending some of his muchachos to get to closer grips with the cowhands below.

Ki gave a concerned "Ahh," to himself, but it acted like a signal to Sweetwater. Two shots roared as one, and two bandidos went down. With startled yells and curses, the other outlaws leaped to defend their flank, returning the fire. Within moments four more bandidos had been dropped in their tracks. A couple more were threshing and groaning. The rest beat a hasty retreat.

Immediately Ki sprinted in pursuit. Sweetwater panted along beside him. They reached the lip of the crest in time to meet the attack of still more bandidos headed by the giant Luiz Zugate. Few of the bandit rifles were now firing into the cleft at the Mashed-O crew. Sweetwater flashed Ki a fuck-'em grin as he saw the odds mounting against them.

The bandido fire was wild, both from haste and from confusion caused by the shadows. Ki and Sweetwater were concealed low on the rim. The advancing line of bandidos were lined against the night sky, and their first triumphant rush was blasted apart by the twin salvos of covert rifle fire.

Ki heard Zugate's bull voice maddened by rage and frustration. "Attack! Run over these gringos, leave them all dead in the cleft, you *cretinos!*"

Hastily Ki reloaded his weapons. He could dimly see Sweetwater thumbing bullets into his carbine.

The second advance was slower, charier. Yet Zugate fully intended to slay the two men who had caught his forces by surprise, well aware that the Mashed-O would take swift advantage unless the pair were cut down in short order.

The bandidos worked closer, sniping, crouching low to offer smaller targets. Ki's lips set in a grim, straight line as he glanced from them to the dark, steep slope below. In a moment or two the bandidos would charge and overwhelm them, and there was no sign of support from the Mashed-O.

The attack came with the mad surge that Ki expected, the bandidos yelling and leaping forward with flaming guns. He and Sweetwater braced themselves and their own guns answered back. Bandidos dropped but the rest came on.

Suddenly, without warning, other guns thundered from behind the bandidos. They halted, caught between two fires, milled uncertainly and then scattered for cover in all directions. Luiz Zugate came plunging on, though, leveling his revolvers and tripping their hammers, his face livid with the rage and rancor he harbored toward Ki.

Ki took aim, triggered, but his gun snapped empty. A bullet clipped his vest where it swelled slightly from his hand thrusting inside, and a second wild shot past his shoulder brought a cold laugh from between his teeth. The range was long and tricky, but his hand flashed out and moved with precision.

Two slim daggers speared Zugate in the chest and dumped him writhing to the ground. Ki started after him. Zugate did not stay where he had dropped, much to Ki's annoyance. The distance had been a shade too far, the daggers stabbing lethally, but not quite stabbing deep enough to be instantly fatal. Zugate was staggering on saggy legs along the edge of the rimrocks, his face slick with sweat and his eyes dark with defiance. He had a tenacious hold of his revolvers, and as he aimed them, his voice rose rasping above the savage gunfire echoing up from the cleft.

"I am not done wit' this fight, Señor, or wit' you!"

He triggered, his slugs coming amazingly close.

A whirling *shuriken* pierced Zugate and ripped a moan from him. Ki snapped off another, but this one missed as Zugate, buckling, toppled limply over the edge and fell lifeless out of sight.

Behind and below Ki, along the steep bank, could be heard the Mashed-O men climbing toward them. Sweetwater faded into the darkness ahead, emboldened to search for the scattering enemy, who in turn were demoralized by the loss of their leader. Somewhere beyond them the mysterious guns still boomed, and Ki counted three of them. He swiftly reloaded and headed in their direction, catching up with Sweetwater at the verge of the hill. They abruptly halted when they saw three figures loom out of the darkness on the rim across the narrow cleft. Sweetwater shouldered his carbine.

"Ki! Sweetwater! That you over there?" a familiar voice called.

Amazement made Sweetwater drop his carbine. "Jefuckin'hozaphat!"

"Jessie?" Ki laughed with relief. "Are you okay?"

"Dandy. Wade Duval and Prudence are here, too. They're fighting fools."

There was no quick, easy way across the intervening gap, but word alone that their boss and the others were alive, if not entirely safe, heartened the Mashed-O. Courageous before when attacked by the bandidos, the crewmen were ferocious now in dishing out retribution. The bandidos fought like the cornered rats they were, but they could withstand just so much punishment. Most were caught in the crush, but a few were able to escape by scurrying, crawling, battling from the cleft.

One such was Felipe Murillo.

Jessie had been keeping her eyes peeled for Murillo,

especially following the downfall of Luiz Zugate. Now, for the first time, she saw Murillo along with the night-bleared silhouette of gunhand scrambling over the rimrock on her side of the cleft. Suddenly the gunhand let out a piercing scream. Jessie realized that the figure she had mistaken for a man was actually trim, pants-clad Prudence being hauled along bodily by Murillo—that Murillo was again kidnapping her in his desperate bid for freedom.

Apparently spotting the abduction as well, Wade Duval came recklessly charging from his position farther along the rim. Bullets followed, for though the battle had lost its initial savage punch, there was still deadly skirmishing going on. He went down as if hit by a sledge.

"Wade!" Jessie called, momentarily stymied, torn by indecision.

Pulling himself to one knee, Duval clung to a boulder with one hand, the other clutching his chest. He'd been hit high in his pectorals, blood soaking through his shirt and running across his hands, wet and turgid. "I'm aw'ri'. Get after Murillo, afore he drags Pru to wherever their horses are hidden and makes his getaway!"

"But—"

Duval cussed. "Get the hell after him. I'll cover you from here. Go on, it's Pru's only chance!"

No time to hesitate. Duval had raised his carbine again and was pumping the lever, spraying a stream of lead into the surrounding rocks, trying to drive the bandidos away and down. Jessie swung from cover and plunged in the direction Murillo had taken. Half a dozen slugs ripped after her, and one unfortunate shot struck her carbine, perhaps shielding her from serious injury, but ruining the trigger mechanism in the process.

Flinging the carbine aside, Jessie plunged over the far brow of the rim. The other side descended steeply for about thirty feet to a sheltered hollow where, presumably, the bandidos had cavvied their horses. Jessie dashed headlong down the uneven slope and hit bottom with stones and dirt showering about her. Bouldered slabs of rock gave concealment from the hollow, but they blocked her vision as well. Here of course there was no help from Duval. She had ceased hearing a rifle from his position, though, and feared that probably his wound had finished him.

The thought of his death steeled her resolve. Drawing her pistol, Jessie eased between the rocks where mesquite had taken root and grew in dwarf clumps. She could hear movement just ahead, and Murillo's voice . . .

"You're being a fool," he was saying, "if you expect your *gauchos* to fight their way through in time."

"L-let go of me," came Prudence's voice.

Closer now Jessie could tell Murillo was holding Pru, and that she was struggling to wrest free. Jessie boosted herself onto a low, flattish boulder and peered into the black well of the hollow, gaining only a vague impression of the two amongst the dark bulk of horses, then heard Prudence cry out as Murillo spun around.

She dived from the boulder. At the last instant she caught an impression of Murillo's form and changed direction. She slammed the man waist high, carrying him back against a stone cluster. Rebounding, Murillo tore himself to one side, freeing one hand, going for his double-gun.

But Prudence, screaming, pounced on his his arm. Her unexpected ferocity forced his arm wide, and his finger accidently triggered one barrel, firing a bullet that hammered chunks from an adjacent rock. Pru clung with a wild animal strength. Murillo swore in a shrill howl of rage. He braced his legs and hurled her with all his wiry might.

Prudence was torn free, sent flying across the hollow. She struck a horse and went down, clipped by a forehoof, stunned, sitting, one leg bent under her, head forward, hair falling in masses across her lap.

Murillo wheeled back with the smoking double-gun.

Jessie was smiling coldly, her pistol in hand, cocked and pointed.

"No! Not to shoot!" Dropping his gun as if it were burning his fingers, Murillo backed against the stone cluster, his gaze fixed on the pistol centered on his heart. "No, señorita, no. I'm through—"

"You sure are," Jessie said softly.

"Hear me. I'll stop the fighting now. I'll call my *compañeros* to stop," he begged, his face repulsive with terror. "I'll take them south. Over the Sierra Madre. You'll never hear of us again, I prom—"

Staggering bootsteps sounded behind Jessie. She spun around. It was Luiz Zugate, wavering like some ghastly visage from the grave, bleeding from dagger and *shuriken* wounds, his features crushed and battered from his fall. By all rights he should have been dead, but the huge *bandido* was beyond knowing or caring about that, existing on pure hatred as he leveled his twin revolvers.

"Toss it," he grunted.

Jessie thrust her pistol away with an outflung hand. Defiantly she set herself, heels wide on the rocky ground, thumbs hooked on her belt on either side of her buckle, almost touching her concealed derringer.

Murillo laughed, a sudden wild tremelo. "Luiz, *el maton*—the tough one. Shoot her low, Luiz. Let her kick and squirm for a while."

"No, Felippe. Not for her. She take it in the breast, a bullet from each gun through each nipple. That's how *la Hija de Satanas*—the daughter of Satan—should take her death."

His fingers tensed on the triggers, but something hit Zugate, spinning him to one side. The sound of a Winchester came a fragment of time later. Sound of it seemed impersonal through the thick barrier of boulders.

The high-speed bullet had smashed cleanly through Zugate's left shoulder and down through his chest, exiting to thud into the dirt. His eyes were open, staring, revolvers dangling limply in his fingers. With eyes still gazing straight ahead he folded backward to the ground.

Jessie knew, downright gut knew. It was Brazos Chaldeen, a parting shot from someplace in the dark recesses of the surrounding slopes.

Murillo seemed stunned for an instant. Then he sprang toward his double-gun, snatching it up and twisting around, crouching . . . Jessie had anticipated the move. She whipped out her hidden derringer, fired once. The slug drilled Murillo in the chest. He reeled back on bowed legs, arms lifted shoulder-high. His head and shoulders struck a horse and he lurched off-balance, still gripping the gun in his hand, cocked, but lacking the life to pull the trigger. Her derringer exploded again. Murillo stumbled sideways, took a step going down, and ended head foremost against a boulder.

Jessie strode over, looked down on him. He was dead. Next she went and made sure Zugate had finally expired. Prudence had risen and was holding the horse for support. She was still dizzy from the kick she had taken. She made no resistance when Jessie slipped an arm around her waist for support and led her out of the hollow, back toward the rimrocks.

Bandidos were fleeing on foot along the steep, rugged slopes. A nest of them still cached at the cleft were putting up a defensive fire while Mashed-O crewmen edged closer.

Jessie saw Ki and Sweetwater approaching down the bank, having crossed the cleft as fast as they could. With them was Duval, one arm dangling from the bullet wound in his shoulder.

"Murillo?" Ki asked when they met.

"Dead. And Zugate," she replied, explaining.

Ki shook his head, marveling at Zugate's stamina. "Reminds me of an old Japanese saying," he remarked, "that born killers take a lot of killing."

★

Chapter 12

The fight soon ended and the Mashed-O crew gathered their rustled cattle from the vallecito. There were also, in the cleft, the dead to bury and the injured to tend, including Wade Duval. At length it was all done and, bone-weary yet elated, they drove the retrieved herd back across the border.

There was a suspicious grayness, the false dawn in the sky by the time they reached Mooneye Valley. Despite their exhaustion, Jessie prevailed upon Ki and Prudence to accompany her into the gorge. Wade Duval insisted on going along, his arm bandaged and rigged in a makeshift sling, and Sweetwater felt he should be included, now that Pru had appointed him foreman and the herd was on home range.

Her exclaiming companions followed Jessie down the stream and around the shoulders of rock to the little stretch of beach. From there she led them up the gorge wall and along the secretive trough of a path, constantly searching the surrounding Espantosa Hills with her keen gaze. No sign of life was to be seen, however, and they continued their ride until they arrived at the shelf of rock in the gloomy chasm. Dismounting, they stared in astonishment at the strange gleaming pool in the depths of the fumarole.

"It ain't water, is it?" Sweetwater asked dubiously.

Jessie smiled. "No, it's not water. It's free mercury—quicksilver. Those reddish cliffs are banded with cinnabar, the ore of mercury. Globules of mercury are occasionally found in cinnebar deposits. This is the case here. Through untold ages the globules have been seeping through fissures in the rock and depositing in the fumarole to form the pool."

"Tiz true," Duval confirmed. "Cinnabar is the result of volcanic action. It may be seen in process of formation in hot springs in California and Nevada. Such vein forming activities often reach the surface in fumaroles like this one."

"This was the Abode of the Mirror that Smokes," Jessie explained, "the deity Texcatlipoca of the Aztecs and Toltecs, to which they offered sacrifices. And it's the reason the outlaws hereabouts have been trying to keep everybody off this section till they could scheme some way to gain control of it themselves. You all know how mercury is used in silver and gold mining, but it's also used in the making of drugs, chemicals, explosives, and so on. There's no telling how deep that pool is, but the main value of the deposit is those cinnabar veins in the cliffs."

She ushered her astounded companions across the shelf to the stone table of sacrifice. They examined it, fingered it, passed around back of it and peered into the holes through which the blood of the sacrificial victims had been drained off.

Glancing again at the fumarole, Prudence commented, "Seeing how the pool is so shiny and fuming, it's understandable that the Aztecs worshipped here to a god called the Mirror that Smokes. But I always thought they and the Toltecs lived much farther to the south, way down in the valley of Mexico.''

"They did," Jessie said. "But there's reason to believe that the Aztecs were migrants from the ancient Anasazi cities of what is now New Mexico and Arizona. According to their own legend, they began their wanderings about 1168, and it's quite conceivable they'd have gone this far east as well as south. This would seem to confirm such a theory."

"The big secret," Sweetwater marveled. "The secret everybody has been hunting for decades, and you alone just happenstance across it. Ain't that a flabbergaster.''

"I didn't find it accidently, and I'm not the only one, either," Jessie replied. "The old Yaquis knew of it, for instance, from the descendents of the Aztecs. They tried to keep it secret as a sacred spot and, no doubt, for the hidden pathway that allowed them to sneak north of the border on raids. The prospector from whom Zed Rykoff bought the spread had to've discovered it, too, because he'd drawn a map"—Jessie took out of her pocket the rough copy she had obtained from Rykoff—"which is what led me to locate the place.''

"But nobody could decipher the map," Prudence argued.

"They couldn't read the key." Jessie spread out the map on the table. "Remember, the prospector drew it so he wouldn't forget. Of course he knew the central line here referred to the gorge, but it took me some searching till I found the contact between sedimentary and igneous rock at the strip of beach.''

"Y'mean this symbol here?" Duval asked. "Geologically it stands for a contact, with the wavy lines indicating shale. Is that the key you mean?''

"Yes, that and the two picks drawn at the bottom.''

"Danged if I can see what those tell," Sweetwater grumped.

"Notice the picks each have points A and B marked on

177

them. Obviously they must refer to two points on the map. Looking at it, there are only two possible points—the tops of the two mountains, so let's mark the first one A and the second one B." Jessie made these marks on the map. "The next thing is to find where point A and point B on the first pick line up with the mountains when we sight along the lines made with the handle. That turns out to be at the contact, or rather, at the rim directly above it. The spot where the mountaintops appear as indicated on the second pick, with A over the left point and B over the right point, is the mercury deposit here where you're standing."

"I'll be!" Pru exclaimed. "Well, what's this 3210 mean?"

"Not what it looks like. The prospector had sloppy writing or maybe he penned the 0 too big on purpose, but it's not a zero. It's supposed to be a small o, a degree sign. Three hundred and twenty-one degrees, which is north-westerly, which is the direction taken by the hidden trail." Jessie drew the line of the pathway, completing the solution.

While they were thus occupied, some slight sound, or a presentiment of danger, caused Ki to turn.

Men were streaming out onto the shelf from the other, far mouth of the pathway. Heading a half-dozen hardcase characters were the glowering Big Nick Tualatin and Leo Frost.

Ki's hands streaked to his vest. Two swiftly loosened *shuriken* stabbed one oncoming gunnie in the chest and ripped through the throat of the man close alongside, even as they started firing. The four at the table dived crouching behind the stonework, whipping up their pistols and answering the attack.

Big Nick Tualatin took a bead on Jessie. An instant before he triggered, her bullet glanced off his belt buckle and tore up through his belly, dropping the mine owner on his back, writhing, hands clawing his shirtfront. Another man gave a strangled cry, reeled, and fell. The others dashed onward, yelling and shooting, Leo Frost zigzagging in the forefront, smiling in his old easy way, his revolver blazing.

Ki sprang around the table in a charging tackle.

Frost's revolver thundered next to his face. Ki felt the shock wave of exploding gunpowder and the burn of lead across his cheek, then heard the gun click empty as he closed with the mine superintendent. Frost dropped his gun, his hand lashed out and long, steel-hard fingers clutched Ki by the throat.

Ki found himself battling less of a man than a tenacious animal. Prying on the corded wrist, his left hand slashing in disabling chops, he tried to break Frost's mercilessly choking grip. But Frost buried his head in Ki's chest and unrelentingly held on, his momentum shoving Ki backward.

His senses weakening, Ki felt one of his feet sliding off the edge of the shelf. He wavered, having to compensate for himself and the man who was strangling the life out of him. He regained his foothold, kneed Frost in the groin, and managed to tear his throat free of the abruptly slackening grasp, then jackknifed his body forward, his shoulder striking Frost shin-high. Frost hinged, folding over him, and before the superintendent could recover and latch on to him again, Ki rolled away and stopped at the very brink of the shelf. Frost vaulted over his back and plunged, twisting and turning, down into the fumarole. With a wailing cry of agony and despair, he struck the pool.

The gleaming surface depressed, there was a slow, surging wave and Leo Frost vanished forever. The Mirror that Smokes had claimed its last sacrifice.

Panting, Ki rose and leaned against the table. Around on the shelf he could see the last of the outlaws were down, retching out life on the rocky floor. Big Nick Tualatin was still squirming, but going fast.

Slowly Ki walked across to Jessie, and joined the others gathering around the dying mine owner. Big Nick Tualatin glared back at them with glazing, hate-filled eyes, and with his last expiring breath he gasped out:

"You—got—El Cascabel."

Bewildered, Duval glanced up from his dead employer. "Him? He . . . ?"

"No," Jessie replied. "Tualatin was just a hired hand, though he posed as a mine owner. The long-sought Mexican rattlesnake is down there in that infernal pool of mercury. Leo Frost was actually El Cascabel."

"How on earth did you figure that out?" Pru asked.

"If it hadn't been for your father moving over here, the odds are nobody would've tumbled to him," Ki responded. "But when Frost tried to wideloop a herd that was traildrove worthless to a rustler, he tipped his hand."

"Right then we were sure of what we already suspected," Jessie explained, "that somebody wanted to keep folks from settling on this land. There had to be a reason for it, so we started looking for the reason, and I found it here. Ki first got to thinking about Frost from the way he scratched his matches."

"The way he scratched his matches?"

Ki nodded. "Frost was supposed to've lived all his life in rough mining camps. But I noticed that whenever he scratched a match, he raised his foot and scatched it on the sole of his boot, a funny thing for a miner wearing corduroy pants to do. That's the trick of a city dude who's used to wearing good clothes. Match heads don't hurt corduroys, but they leave streaks on nice trousers. Moreover, Gotch-Ear Gillespie told us how Frost kept a gambler from knifing Tualatin by grabbing his wrist with such force that the knifer had to drop his blade. Well, the night of the first raid, a rustler got me by the wrist and for a minute I thought he'd broken it. It reckoned there couldn't be two men in one district with a grip like that."

"Cigarettes helped tie things onto Frost, too," Jessie added. "Frost was a chain smoker, lighting one quirly after another, especially when excited or interested in something he was doing. Look around, you'll see cigarette butts littering the shelf here.'' She made a sweeping gesture with her arm, going on to say, ''Oh, Frost knew about mining, all right. Down in Mexico, El Cascabel had lots of Yaqui Indians riding with him, and I imagine he got the story of the Mirror that Smokes from one of them. Knowing mining, it didn't take him long to figure out what it meant. He came up here and found the mercury deposit, but Zed Rykoff had already got title to the land. So he began scheming to get it away from Rykoff. He began mining low-grade silver ore in the hills to give him and maybe some of his gang members cover for hanging around the area. Maybe he didn't have the ready cash to buy the land from Rykoff, or, what's more likely, he figured it would look suspicious for a mining superintendent to go buying a cattle spread and might make Rykoff wonder why and try to find out. Also, chances are he figured he couldn't measure up to what Rykoff wanted for a neighbor. So he set out to keep folks off the land until Rykoff got disgusted and would be ready to sell out to anyone, or until he, Frost, had lined up somebody he had control of who could satisfy Rykoff's requirements.''

''Well, he lined up Yarbrough,'' Sweetwater grumbled. ''Still, I don't savvy. Didn't he kinda help you, Ki, and help kill Yarbrough?''

''Had no choice,'' Ki answered. ''Yarbrough bungled the attempt, and Frost couldn't risk plugging me without getting nailed himself. So he took the smart way and besides, Yarbrough was a liability by then, wounded or not.''

''Vaughn Yarbrough wasn't really working for Frost, not directly,'' Jessie said. ''Frost didn't get here until a couple of years back. Yarbrough wouldn't have had time to be approached and sell out when he arrived with the Mashed-O, so he must've gotten to know Murillo and Zugate a long time ago, when he first came through the Big Bend country. So they're the ones he spied for, and they in turn worked in a loose-knit partnership with Frost.''

''More loose than knit,'' Ki added. ''They operated like knife fighters in a scarf duel—staying tied together while looking to stick it to each other. Frost cut Zugate and Murillo out of the first raid, so they retaliated by sticking up his Fortuna mine and staging the second raid. I doubt they knew Pru was there, any more than they knew of the mercury here, but they would've known she and her spread were worth plenty to Frost.''

''Now I catch what Mad Knecht was babbling about,'' Duval remarked. ''He and Brazos Chaldeen were Frost's ace in the hole, to keep tabs on Zugate and Murillo and maybe take over their gang if push came to shove.''

''Yes, and to take the blame as boss of the Espantosa Riders, which was Frost's own band of gringo outlaws on this side of the Rio.'' Jessie waved at the sprawl of dead gunmen. ''Those're the last of his Riders, or darn near.''

Sweetwater scratched his head. ''So Tualatin lied about the posse he was goin' to form, and Frost used the lie as an excuse to skedaddle back, eh?''

''Reckon that's it,'' Ki agreed. ''Frost got Tualatin and whatever men were handy, I'd say, picked up our trail and saw us heading into the gorge. Took a chance on wiping out the lot of us.''

''If you hadn't turned around when you did, I allow that's just what Mr. El Cascabel Frost would've done,'' Pru declared ardently.

Ki pretended not to hear.

''All that's left now, Pru, is to cash in on this deposit,'' Jessie advised. ''Any ideas how you might want to develop it?''

''Why, none at all. Will you help, Jessie? You've certainly earned a share in this.''

But Jessie smilingly shook her head. ''Not me, thanks. I think Starbuck would gladly grubstake your project, though, perhaps for an option to buy the mercury. And I've a hunch there's a mining pro beside you who'd love to help plan and operate the venture.''

"It's like gold," Duval said exuberantly, sliding his good arm around Pru's waist. "Like gold. Red gold. It's something the world needs ten times more than gold! You'll be richer than Midas e'er dreamed of.''

Prudence seemed content to remain as she was, cheek pressed against the rough cloth of Duval's shirt, her hair falling in ringlet masses over his chest.

And Jessie exchanged a knowing glance with Ki, then gazed out across the fumarole. The sunrise was laving the eastern horizon with fire, and the yonder spires of ruddy granite seemed bathed in blood. The monstrous shoulders of the Espantosa Hills were still swathed in purple shadows, from which those bloody crags fanged up into a crimson sky. . . . *A land of red, burnished red, like red gold*, she thought; *a country where strange things have happened and where anything may yet happen. . . .*

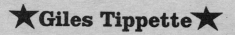